A CHRISTMAS KISS

"Let's see if we can finish what's left of that fudge." Fred laced his fingers through hers and led her toward the kitchen.

When he stopped her under the archway, and his mistletoe trap, Lindsay laughed. But not for long. He caught her in a kiss, and her arms came up around him immediately, her lips both yielding and giving. It was several minutes before he could bring himself to raise his head. Until now he'd never focused on anything but the present, but until now he'd never believed the present could be so eternal. Did she feel even a fraction of what he felt? He looked down into Lindsay's face, and her eyes were bright once more, her cheeks flushed.

Yes. At least a fraction.

"I thought you were after the fudge." Lindsay didn't move one centimeter toward the kitchen, didn't stir from his arms.

"I found something sweeter."

No Christmas Like The Present

SIERRA DONOVAN

ZEBRA BOOKS
KENSINGTON PUBLISHING CORP.
http://www.kensingtonbooks.com

First Printing: October 2014
ISBN-13: 978-1-4201-3420-9
ISBN-10: 1-4201-3420-5

First Electronic Edition: October 2014
ISBN-13: 978-1-4201-3421-6
ISBN-10: 1-4201-3421-3

10 9 8 7 6 5 4 3 2 1

Printed in the United States of America

To Donny and Sierra

You've grown up seeing way too much of the back of your mother's head while she sits in front of a computer. Thank you.

I love you both beyond words.

Acknowledgments

Christmas is all about believing, and this book wouldn't be here without the faith and support of a lot of people. Here are a few of the people who made it possible:

My husband, Charlie, first and foremost, for believing in me always.

Stephanie Newton and Jody Wallace, two of the first people to believe in Fred.

Al Gansky, for leading me to Jonathan Clements, my agent at Wheelhouse Literary Group. Jonathan, for taking me on, and his associate, Annette Marshall, for helping him get this story in front of the right people.

And John Scognamiglio, my editor at Kensington Publishing, for saying "Yes."

Chapter 1

December sixteenth, and she'd barely started on her Christmas cards.

Lindsay Miller sat in the living room of her apartment, the TV tray in front of her stacked high with cards and envelopes. Every year she promised herself she'd get started early, and every year she ended up behind. The whole first paragraph of the notes in her cards used to be an apology for being late, apologies for not writing during the year, and pledges to do better next year. At twenty-nine, she'd given up on the annual litany of excuses. They'd heard it too many times before. But every year, she still vowed to herself that she'd surprise them all.

Next year.

Lindsay sighed and brushed a handful of light brown hair behind her ear again as she bent to her task. She flipped her worn vinyl address book to the *G's*. Only the seventh letter of the alphabet.

Out of the corner of her eye, she sneaked another glance at the old black-and-white version of *A Christmas Carol* they were showing on television. It was her favorite scene, as Scrooge's jolly nephew Fred once again explained the joys of Christmas to his uncle. And it was her favorite version of the film, because this Fred was exceptionally handsome. Elegant and dark-haired, with warm dark eyes and exquisite features, resplendent in his long, trim overcoat, top hat in hand.

"I have always thought of Christmas time as a good time," he said in his rich voice, with that cultured British accent. *"The only time I know of when men and women seem, by one consent, to open their shut-up hearts freely. . . ."*

Right, Lindsay thought wryly. *Just as soon as I finish these cards.*

But she felt a pang. Another holiday season was passing by. She'd gotten her packages sent, at least, but she still had more shopping to do . . . more batches of fudge to make . . . and these cards . . . all to fit around eight hours a day at the office. To really do it right, she had a feeling Christmas would be a full-time job in itself.

She pulled her eyes away from Fred and brought her attention back to the next name in the address book. Ruth Gillespie. Her old college roommate. When was the last time they'd talked? She made the annual mental vow to call her in January, once the holiday rush had passed.

As Fred stubbornly wished Scrooge a Merry Christmas and a happy New Year, Lindsay's doorbell rang. She checked the pendulum clock hanging on the living room wall. Almost seven P.M. During the summer, when it was still light outside, she wouldn't have thought twice about someone coming to the door at this hour, but now that it was well after dark, it gave her pause.

Frowning, she approached the door and tried to peer out the peephole. No good. She'd decorated her door with gift wrap the first week of December, when she still had hopes of getting Christmas right this year. Reluctantly, Lindsay opened the door about twelve inches, her hand still clutching the knob, and peered out.

It was Fred.

The same Fred she'd just seen on television, from a movie made over fifty years ago.

Lindsay turned to check the TV screen, and there stood Fred, framed in the door of Scrooge's counting house. She turned back to her visitor, framed in her own doorway, and blinked. Hard. The same long, slender overcoat. The same top hat. And the same handsome face, down to the ready smile and the glimmer in his eye. Except that this Fred was in living color.

He removed his hat, revealing a head of wavy dark hair that did nothing to lessen the resemblance.

"Miss Lindsay Miller?" he said, and his voice even held the same trace of a British accent. Not the kind of accent you heard every day here in Lakeside, Colorado.

Eyes didn't *twinkle* in real life. And they certainly couldn't dance. The very thought was corny beyond belief. Or at least Lindsay would have thought so. This man's eyes appeared to be doing both, and while it made her stomach flip, it wasn't from nausea. But what was with the nineteenth-century getup? He must be a walking advertisement for one of those chimney-sweeping services. Someone should tell him the fireplaces in this apartment complex were all the ornamental, natural-gas kind.

Somehow, he knew her name. Maybe it was a singing telegram. Who would send her a singing telegram?

She tightened her grip on the doorknob. "Yes? What can I do for you?"

"For me? Not a thing. I was sent here strictly for your benefit."

It had to be a sales pitch, or worse. Lindsay steeled herself against the laughing eyes that gleamed at her under her porch light. "I'm sorry," she said, and started to close the door. "I'm not interested in buying anything tonight—"

A smooth black walking stick jutted out, blocking the swing of the door. A walking stick?

"No, no, Miss Miller, you misunderstand. I came because I was told you've been missing out on the spirit of Christmas—"

That did it. He was crazy. Lindsay shoved harder against the walking stick and slammed the door. The stick got stuck in the doorjamb, and she froze in alarm; then, mercifully, it slid back outside, and she shut the door the rest of the way. She leaned her shoulder against the door as she first bolted it, then turned the lock on the knob, then resolved to get one of those security chains. And never to answer her door again after dark.

She started toward the phone in the kitchen, ready to call the police if the strange man outside gave her any more trouble.

She got halfway to the kitchen before she nearly walked into him. He stood in the middle of her apartment, right where the living room led into the kitchen.

It couldn't be. A scream tried to make its way out of her throat, but her breath stuck in her windpipe. How in the world had he gotten in?

He took a step back and held up his hands in front of him, as if to show he meant no harm. The walking stick dangled loosely between his fingers. Halfway down, it was slightly bent, as if it had been slammed in someone's front door.

"Please," he said, "give me just a moment. We've gotten off to a bad start."

His dark eyes looked absolutely guileless, but that didn't lessen her alarm. He stood between her and the kitchen phone, her lifeline to the sane world. Maybe she could get her hands on a weapon.

Lindsay cast her eyes furtively in search of a blunt instrument. "You're breaking and entering."

"Nonsense. I haven't *broken* anything." He held the walking stick out to her, still hanging it loosely from his fingertips. "Here. Take this, if it makes you feel better. All I ask is that you hear me out."

She snatched the stick and thought about cracking him over the head with it, but his steady gaze was so far from menacing, somehow she couldn't. Instead, she angled the walking stick toward him, reinforcing the distance between them. "Who gave you my name?" She started to sidle around him, toward the phone.

"That's a little hard to explain. I was sent by my supervisors." He maneuvered, too, always a safe distance away, but still keeping himself between her and the phone. His words came a little faster. "Miss Miller—may I call you Lindsay?"

She didn't answer. They'd nearly reached the countertop where the phone rested, and he stood in front of it.

"You're missing out on the most wonderful season life has to offer. And I'm here to help."

She switched tactics, tentatively advancing toward him with the stick extended. He backed away. Whatever else he might be, he didn't seem aggressive—or, at least, not physically violent. Although he was every bit as stubbornly persistent as Scrooge's nephew.

He went on, "You spend every Christmas rushing to get things done, without ever stopping to enjoy it. You know there's more to be gotten out of Christmas, and every year you try to find it. That's why I'm here."

With the help of the prodding stick, Lindsay reached the white tile counter. She groped for the phone, never taking her eyes away from the stranger in front of her.

"Lindsay, you need my help." Her searching hand knocked over the jar of pens next to the phone, and continued to fumble for the handset. He started to tick items off on long, slender fingers. "You've spent the past week making batch after batch of fudge to send to your aunts, uncles and cousins. You spent the rest of that same week organizing the children's choral performance at the community center—which I understand was lovely, by the way. You're drowning in a hideous stack of cards for people who never hear from you the rest of the year. You have a carton of eggnog in your refrigerator that expires in two days, and you haven't even opened it."

She didn't remember the date on the eggnog, but she knew she hadn't opened it yet. Her skin crawled. He'd been in her apartment, had gone through her things, and he'd been watching her. That was the only explanation. Lindsay seized the phone.

"And when you were ten years old, you peeked at your biggest Christmas present, but you never did it again because it spoiled the surprise."

She almost dropped the handset. No one knew that. Not even her parents.

He added, "A tape recorder, I believe."

Impossible. He must have found out somehow.

Lindsay firmed her grip on the cordless handset and turned it on. But when she raised the phone to her ear, she didn't hear a dial tone. Instead, soft strings played "I Heard the Bells on Christmas Day." Lindsay squeezed the phone hard, and the room swam as if she were seeing it through a wet pane of glass.

She glanced up at her strange visitor. He regarded her quietly, still a safe distance away, although she'd forgotten to brandish the walking stick.

Lindsay switched the phone off, then back on. This time she heard "It Came Upon a Midnight Clear."

In addition to everything else, apparently, he knew her two favorite carols.

She stared at him numbly. "How did you do that?"

The swirling room darkened to black, and she barely felt the arms that caught her before she could hit the floor.

When Lindsay opened her eyes, she found herself slumped half-upright on the sofa. Her strange intruder knelt in front of her, both of her hands in his. He was rubbing her wrists together, his brows bent downward in diligent concentration.

He glanced up, and the frown cleared. "There you are. I'm afraid I gave you a bit of a turn."

His smile reached all the way to his eyes, and she reminded herself that either he was crazy, or she was hallucinating.

"You may be an undigested bit of beef," Scrooge's voice told Marley's ghost from the television set across the room. *"A blot of mustard. A fragment of an underdone potato."*

But the hands that held hers felt solid enough, and warm enough. The dark brown eyes that studied her seemed full of concern. She should be afraid. But somehow, as she looked into those eyes, an odd calm washed over her. She felt confused. A little dizzy. But not afraid.

She forced her gaze away from his eyes, to study the rest of his face. The elegant cheekbones, the firm mouth . . . he really did look for all the world like Scrooge's nephew from the film. Which put her own sanity in doubt as much as his. Unless she woke up soon and found out this was all a dream, she'd better call a doctor and get a CAT scan or something.

Under her stare, the laughing light in his eyes gave way to a more serious look. "They were supposed to put me into a form that would appeal to you. Did they do all right?"

That went way beyond the realm of fishing for a compliment. Lindsay had no idea how to answer it. Instead, she said, "Who are 'they'?"

"My supervisors. At Headquarters. You see, I have a job to do. A very pleasant one, actually. I get to show you how to enjoy Christmas."

She tried to pull herself up straight, but another wash of dizziness swam through her head. This time she refused to black out.

"You know, you look like you could use some of that eggnog right about now." He gave her hands a squeeze as he started to rise.

"Wait." She had to get this man out of her apartment and reclaim her sanity. But first, she wanted some answers. "How did you know about the eggnog? And the tape recorder?"

"It's my job to know." He cradled her hands in both of his, not tightly. It would have been easy to pull away if she tried. But his voice was so earnest and soothing, an unlikely stillness lingered over her, along with the illogical conviction that he couldn't mean her any harm.

What was he doing to her? She should have thwacked him with that walking stick while she had the chance.

"You see, Lindsay, you put so much *work* into Christmas that you miss out on the joy. And isn't that what those cards and presents are for? How can you *share* joy with the people around you, if you don't experience it yourself? You work so hard that you forget to give the most important gift of all. You're not giving of yourself. And from where I sit, they're missing out on a lot."

"It is required of every man that the spirit within him should walk abroad among his fellow men," Marley's ghost intoned.

"You don't know me," she said.

"I know you better than you think. I know what I need to know for right now. The rest, I can learn as I go. More fun that way." He eyed the TV tray full of cards, next to him on the living room floor. "So, what's left to do, besides all those cards?"

That funny calm wouldn't leave her. She said, "More fudge."

"You've got to be joking. You must have made fifteen pounds of that stuff by now."

He was probably right. "I need more for my friends at work. Then there's the rest of the shopping."

"And would the world come to an end if you told your friends 'Merry Christmas' instead of making another batch of fudge?"

"I've done it every year."

He shook his head. "You see, that's the kind of thinking you need to let go of. It's stealing your enjoyment. You don't *have* to do it all, every year, just because of some self-imposed precedent."

Why was she listening to any of this? Lindsay pulled her hands away, and he let go without resisting. The room suddenly seemed colder. But that had to be her imagination.

He stood, brushed off his knees, and said brightly, "Time for that eggnog."

"No, wait." She'd let this go way too far. Lindsay recovered her feet and followed him, on wobbly legs, out to the kitchen. "You have to go."

"Oh, I will." He opened a cabinet. He knew exactly where she kept her holly-patterned mugs, the ones she hadn't used this year since she got them out of their box. "Just let me pour you a cup of cheer before I go. That's what you need."

"I don't want any—"

"Oh, I don't mean that dusty bottle of brandy at the back of your pantry. *That's* not what you need." He opened her refrigerator, where he immediately found the carton of eggnog in the side of the door. "You need—"

"For you to leave." That was a little blunt. Better

to humor him. He might not seem threatening, but standing beside him, she realized he stood at least six feet tall, compared to her five-foot-two. He was slender, but broad-shouldered and solidly built, not someone she wanted to mess with if he suddenly turned on her and had a fit. "I mean," she backpedaled, "this is nice of you, but . . ."

"Don't worry." He opened the eggnog and poured it. "I'm not a psychopath. They don't have those, where I come from."

An image returned to her, of Scrooge's nephew on a snowy London street. "Where's that?"

He shrugged. "Headquarters. You wouldn't find it on any map."

Play along until he leaves. "So you're saying you're, what? An angel?"

"Oh, no. That's far too lofty for me. Just an ordinary messenger." He inclined his head toward the television set in the next room. "Your own personal Spirit of Christmas Present, if you like."

He reached unerringly into her spice cabinet, sprinkled the eggnog with nutmeg, and offered her the mug. "After all, I think it's living in the present that you need the most help with, don't you?"

She accepted the mug with shaky fingers. "I don't know."

"Well, we'll start with that theory. I think the

present is a fine place to start. I spend all of my time there, myself."

He watched her expectantly, then gave an encouraging nod toward the mug in her hand. Lindsay took a sip to humor him. She watched him over the mug and willed him to leave.

"There, that's a start." He stepped back into the living room. Lindsay followed, mug in hand, hoping to see him safely out the door. To her consternation, he stopped halfway through the room. "Now, you really ought to have some more decorations in here, don't you think? Starting with a real tree."

"I already have a tree." She nodded at the three-foot fiber-optic tree she'd bought this year to simplify matters. Something easy to set up and put away, instead of buying a fresh tree to throw away in a few weeks, not to mention digging into the back of the hall closet where all her boxes of lights and ornaments were buried. The little tree sat on the end table between her sofa and love seat, the glowing tips of its needles merging endlessly from red to blue to green to orange.

He scowled. "*That's* not a tree. That's only a tree if you're not physically able to put up a real one. Or if, for some odd reason, it says 'Merry Christmas' to you. Does that tree say 'Merry Christmas' to you?"

"Sure," Lindsay lied.

"Liar," he said amiably, and continued toward the door. Lindsay tried to conceal her sigh of relief.

He picked up his hat and the bent walking stick from the back of the couch, near the front door. With the tall black hat settled jauntily on his head, he was once again the complete image of Scrooge's nephew Fred. An image so appealing, it almost made her sorry to see him go.

Almost.

With his hand on the doorknob, he turned to her again. "So," he said, "what are your plans for tomorrow evening?"

Lindsay's breath caught in her throat. "Nothing. I mean, you've helped me enough." She hefted the nearly full mug of eggnog weakly. "This is great."

"Don't be silly. We've barely begun. So, you say you're free tomorrow?"

"No. I've got—" Lindsay broke off. Something told her it would be a terrible mistake to tell him about the company Christmas party. "I have to work late."

He frowned. Whether he was crazy or a bona fide apparition, even his frown was handsome. "Working late, this close to Christmas? They ought to be ashamed. Well, I'll see you again soon."

Lindsay gulped. "You don't mean at the stroke of midnight or something, do you?"

"Of course not. How rude that would be." He glanced at the television set, then winked at her.

"You can't believe everything you see in films, you know."

And he opened her door and passed through it like any normal human being. Lindsay caught a brief glimpse of the tall, dark figure silhouetted by her porch light before the door closed behind him.

She locked the door. Bolted it. Turned off the porch light. And leaned against it for a moment, the mug of eggnog clutched in her hand.

Finally she staggered the few steps to the couch and sagged into its cushions, setting the mug down on the end table next to the tacky fake Christmas tree. Fleetingly, she wished there really was something stronger in the cup. She stared at the black-and-white screen through glassy eyes. It took some time before the images began to take on meaning again.

When the haze cleared, Fred was entertaining his Christmas guests, imitating Scrooge with that inextinguishable good-natured light in his eyes. He led his visitors in a laughing chorus of "*Bah, humbug!*"

Lindsay reached for her mug and drank another sip of the eggnog she hadn't taken the time to sample until tonight. She couldn't begin to explain what had just happened. But the old familiar flavor of the sweet drink soothed her, and brought back an undeniable taste of Christmas.

Chapter 2

What was it about mingling? Lindsay wondered.

She stood in her bosses' living room, making small talk with Nikki and Frank, two of her co-workers. At a get-together like this, she always felt tongue-tied, almost as if someone had her by the throat. She saw these people every day. Why was it so hard to find something to say now? Maybe because they'd all transformed in the last hour and a half, changing from the business-casual clothing they wore at the office into actual suits, ties and dressier dresses. Lindsay hadn't worn this satiny, champagne-colored dress before tonight; that might be another reason she didn't feel quite like herself.

The group broke up, and she turned, looking for someone else to talk to. Right now, the twenty or so employees of Newmeyer and Associates had all formed clusters in Phil and Evelyn Newmeyer's big living room, the scene of all three of the company holiday parties since Lindsay had worked for the couple's small firm. "Living room" was a misnomer. This was clearly an entertaining room, with a long table loaded down with food, and lots of empty floor space in the middle for standing and chatting. She wondered what it looked like the rest of the year. She'd never seen the room without those big swoops of pine garland running across all four walls.

Rather than find her way to the edge of another one of the groups, she decided to take a breather and sample the hors d'oeuvre table. Phil and Evelyn always put out a tempting assortment of snacks and desserts, and there ought to be fresh material for conversation there. *Isn't this great brie?*

She'd taken one step toward the long table at the other end of the room when she heard a rich male voice, the texture of suede, at her elbow: "Ah, there you are."

Lindsay felt the blood run to her toes at the sound of the pleasant British accent. By this morning, she'd all but convinced herself that last night had been a dream. Now this.

She sucked in her breath and turned slowly around to face last night's Christmas visitor.

If he was smug about catching her at the company holiday party, rather than slaving at her desk the way she'd implied, his smile barely hinted at it.

"How'd you get in?" she asked.

His eyes sparkled with infuriating merriment. "Why, through the front door, like everyone else."

Lindsay glanced around furtively. Had Phil or Evelyn actually let him in, or had he just popped in, materialized, the way he had in her apartment last night? Probably not, since everyone stood in the same groups as before, with no bewildered eyes staring their way. A hideous thought occurred to her. What if he really *was* a figment of her imagination? For all she knew she was standing here in front of everyone, talking to empty space. She might end up spending Christmas in the loony bin.

"Can they see you?" she whispered.

"Of course. I told you, you watch too many movies."

Lindsay shifted her weight from one high heel to the other. How to get him out of here? Heaven only knew what he might say to her coworkers. "You're not supposed to be here," she hissed.

"What? Not presentable enough? I did away with the hat for tonight. It didn't seem to be what people are wearing these days."

The period clothing. She hadn't thought about that. Lindsay gave him a hasty once-over. Men's fashions didn't change as much as women's, and without the long overcoat, his simple black suit coat and vest didn't look too out of place. In fact, they accentuated his broad shoulders and trim waist nicely, but that wasn't the issue here. The

19

elaborately ruffled white shirt, and the oversize bow tie . . .

"The shirt and tie are a little too—" She broke off. "It doesn't matter. You have to go."

"Go? But I just got here." His calm was maddening. "You look wonderful, by the way."

Lindsay ignored the warm flush in her cheeks and cast her eyes around as if the walls or furniture held some answer, some quick and quiet way out of this.

"You could tell everyone I'm an imposter and make a scene," he suggested. "But that wouldn't be much fun. Why not give me a chance? I promise to be a perfect gentleman."

"Lindsay." A bright, cheery female voice behind Lindsay sealed her fate. "I didn't know you were bringing someone. Who's this?"

Well, people could see him, all right. Lindsay turned to find her friend Jeanne, dressed to the nines in a classic little black dress. Lindsay felt a brief flicker of hope. If she could catch the woman's eye, give her some signal that everything was not right—

It was no use. The pretty blonde's eyes were riveted on Fred. From the appreciative look on her face, she found him every bit as appealing as Lindsay had—when he'd been in his proper place, on the small screen in her living room.

Playing "normal" seemed like the only thing left to do. "Jeanne, this is—"

Lindsay's mind went blank; she had no idea what to call him. She said the only name that came into her mind: "Fred."

Glancing toward her uninvited escort, she was gratified to see his brows twitch in the faintest of frowns. "Fred . . ." Her mind fumbled. "Holliday."

"Delighted," he said. The frown vanished. Taking Jeanne's hand, he inclined his head toward Lindsay slightly, as if prompting her. Prompting her to do what?

Oh. "Fred, this is Jeanne Weber."

At least it got him to let go of her hand. Jeanne was positively beaming, and for some reason that irked Lindsay. Why? Jeanne was sweet, her closest friend in the office. The fact that she could have her pick of any male in the room wasn't her fault.

"How did you two meet?" Jeanne asked. She didn't seem puzzled by Fred's style of dress, Lindsay realized. Then she noticed he was now wearing a much more understated, contemporary white shirt, with a simple, slim black bow tie. *When did that happen?*

"I'm here visiting," Fred said to Jeanne. "A friend told me I should look Lindsay up. I'm so glad I did." He turned a smile her way, and Lindsay felt another absurd flush. His words seemed directed at her alone, as if they shared a lovely secret.

"She's showing me her way of keeping the Christmas season. I hope I'm not intruding."

"Oh, not at all." Jeanne's smile widened. "I could listen to your accent all night. What part of England are you from?"

"Camden." He slipped a hand gently under Lindsay's elbow, and she managed not to jump. "You know, dear, I owe Lindsay a trip to the punch bowl. Catch up with you later?"

At Jeanne's glowing nod, he steered Lindsay toward the refreshment table. "What kind of a name is 'Fred,' anyway?" he murmured to her out of the corner of his mouth.

"You weren't helping. It was the first thing I could come up with."

"But 'Fred'?" He ladled punch into her cup, smiling at her through his teeth.

"Scrooge's nephew."

"Of course. I should have known." He shrugged. "Well, I like the 'holiday' part, anyway." He handed a crystal cup of punch to her.

So now he had a name. Every move she made seemed to draw Lindsay deeper into the quicksand. Her head started to hurt.

A headache. That could actually come in handy. A quick ticket out of here, before "Fred" could do anything strange. "You know," she said, "we should—"

"Lindsay." The sound of her name was like having

manacles slapped on her wrists. This time it came
from her boss, Phil. No chance for a quick or gra-
cious exit here. "Who's your friend?"

Behind his bifocals, Phil regarded Fred with the
same open curiosity. Lindsay opened her mouth,
but Fred was already offering his hand with a
hearty smile. "Fred," he said. "Fred Holliday."

"It's nice to meet you, Fred," Phil said. "Where
are you from?"

A sinking feeling of inevitability settled in her
stomach. As Fred cheerfully held forth with her
boss, Lindsay felt the chance for escape dwindle
away. She tried to interject, but Phil was already
saying, "Let me show you my hobby room."

That did it. Phil separated the world into two
groups of people: the ones he'd already subjected
to his collection of ships in bottles, and those he
hadn't. Everyone else in the room had already
gotten the tour before, but Fred was fair game. A
fresh victim. Before she knew it, Phil was steering
Fred out of the room, and Evelyn—Phil's wife,
Lindsay's other boss—was greeting her.

"Who's your friend?" Evelyn asked. Lindsay
couldn't remember when she'd been the object of
so much attention in such a short time. It might
have a little to do with the fact that she'd never
brought a date to the company party before, but
she knew Fred would have drawn plenty of curiosity no matter what.

As she stammered out a response, Lindsay cast a last desperate glance over Evelyn's silk-clad shoulder at Fred, who turned away from Phil long enough to give her a solemn wink.

Word about Fred spread quickly, and Lindsay discovered that having a handsome British stranger for a party date provided her with an instant conversation piece. She couldn't even get to the brie. Every time she tried, someone else flagged her down with eager questions. Trying to ad-lib the answers didn't do anything for her headache. Neither did her cup of punch, a heady mixture of pineapple juice and 7UP. It didn't contain any alcohol, but it made up for that with its lethal double dose of sugar.

When Phil brought Fred back from the tour, Lindsay tried to get to him. But no. Matt the accountant blocked her way, and over his shoulder, she could see Fred captured by Jeanne.

Fred caught her eye, shrugged, and turned to hear whatever Jeanne was saying. Lindsay felt her blood sizzle, and reminded herself that she'd always liked Jeanne. The point was to get Fred out of here before he said or did something outrageous.

A moment later he started toward her again, but this time Evelyn accosted him.

It went on that way for about twenty minutes. Lindsay wouldn't have guessed a large room with twenty-odd people in it could seem this crowded. Every time she tried to catch up with him, or Fred with her, there always seemed to be a knot of people between them. At this rate he'd know everyone in the office as well as she did before the night was over. As far as she could tell from everyone's comments, at least he hadn't said anything too bizarre.

And then he stood at her elbow, holding out a plate laden with cheese, crackers, a few strawberries, and some decadent-looking chocolate wafers. Somehow *he'd* made it to the refreshment table, darn him. Or maybe one of the women had offered to hand-feed him. "Try the chocolate," he said.

Lindsay bypassed the tempting chocolate and reached for the cheese and crackers, something to ease her headache. Now, if she could just keep him in her sight long enough to escort him quietly out of here. "Fred, we have to—"

"I can see I'm saddled with that name for the duration."

"I've thought of a few worse things to call you."

"You don't mean that. Say, are you all right?"

She felt his eyes on her, and looked into them before she thought. He caught her in a warm, dark gaze, full of the same concern he'd shown after she fainted in her apartment. "You look tired," he said.

"Thanks a lot."

"Sorry. Lovely, but tired. I think you need to sit down."

Cupping her elbow in his hand again, he guided her toward the far side of the room. Lindsay started to protest, then thought better of it. Let him think she was some kind of wilting Victorian flower. This headache was her excuse to leave.

She sat in one of the little-used chairs lined up against the wall. He leaned over her and ran his fingertips lightly over a spot just above her temple. From across the room, it probably looked like a romantic gesture. From where Lindsay sat, it was more than that; her headache eased.

No. It went away. Lindsay shook her head hard, trying to bring it back.

She blinked, wondering if he knew what he'd just done.

"Better?" So he did know.

She stuck to her original purpose. "We need to go."

To her surprise, he didn't argue. "I agree. I don't like you looking pale." He tipped her chin up to look at him. "I wish you'd accept that I'm here to help you, though. What did you think I was going to do, start rattling chains and raving about Spirits of Christmas Past and Present?"

Maybe the overload was wearing her down. Or maybe he really wasn't crazy. Maybe, with his inexplicable entrances and costume changes, he was exactly what he said he was. If not, he almost certainly had to be a member of the Houdini family, and a mind reader to boot.

A smile touched his lips. "You know, the sooner you let me help, the sooner we can start making progress."

"The sooner you'll be gone?" She hadn't thought of it quite that way before.

"Oh, now you've cut me to the quick. I've only known you a little while, and I'll miss you terribly when I'm gone." He was still smiling, but for once, he actually sounded serious.

A dangerous idea began to blossom in her mind, and Lindsay found herself toying with it. He'd shown absolutely no sign that he intended to harm her. Could it be safe to go along with it, just for a little while? She had a feeling she wouldn't be able to shake him any other way.

It couldn't hurt to humor him here, anyway, in a roomful of witnesses. "Okay. What do I need to do?"

"It's a grueling, tedious job, really. Start enjoying yourself. Here, have one of these."

He picked up one of the sinful-looking chocolate wafers and offered it to her. He *would* have to choose the least dietetic thing on the plate.

At least he'd saved some chocolate for her.

Silently, Lindsay reached up and took it, the wheels turning in her head. When she bit into

27

the wafer, it was every bit as rich and decadent as it looked.

This was the part where she should run away screaming.

She'd gotten him out of Phil and Evelyn's house, amid a greater-than-usual number of friendly farewells. Now they walked down the darkened street toward her car, which she'd parked several houses away because of all the arrivals before her. Fred had her hand tucked through his arm in that courtly way of his, and still showed no sign of menace. Screaming seemed silly.

She stole a glance at Fred, who wore nothing warmer than his simple suit jacket. "You don't have your coat."

"I figured I'd be indoors most of the evening. Don't worry. A brisk walk on a chilly night always does me good."

It was more than chilly. The cold air had the harsh bite and gray, indefinable scent of threatening snow. But with her hand tucked into the crook of Fred's arm, Lindsay felt warmer. She noticed the difference when they reached her car, and she disentangled herself to unlock the door. Instantly the wind seemed sharper, colder, harder, and she hurriedly twisted the key with numb fingers.

Not fast enough to keep Fred from pulling the door open for her, though.

Lindsay slipped inside quickly, hoping to escape Fred and the wind at the same time. Inside her car, it didn't feel much warmer than it had outside; she bunched her jacket around her as she reached to pull the door shut.

Fred still held it. He kept it open just a crack, shutting out most of the cold wind, while he leaned down to speak once more. "Good night, Lindsay. Drive safely."

And he closed the door for her.

Well, that had been easy enough. He straightened with a little wave and stepped back to the sidewalk, giving Lindsay room to pull out of her parking space.

She started to drive off, but as her car turned away from the curb, she saw him in her side mirror, hands deep in his pockets, arms gathered in and head slightly bent against the cold as he walked. He didn't look back.

She knew it was freezing out there. She'd been shivering even in her coat. Lindsay would have bet money that it would snow by morning.

She stopped the car, engine still running. *You'll be sorry,* she told herself.

Lindsay pressed the button to roll down the passenger window, letting in a slice of biting wind. "Fred?" He lifted his head and stepped toward her window. "Where's your car?"

"Oh, I don't drive."

Of course not.

"Oh." She should drive away now. But it was so cold. "Can I—give you a lift anywhere?" She couldn't believe she was saying it.

"You could drop me off over by the Broadway Hotel." He smiled at her through the opening in her window. "As long as it's no trouble, that is."

She usually avoided Lakeside Boulevard because it was in such a busy section of town, but in reality, it was the shortest route home. And this time of night, the traffic wouldn't be bad.

She should pull away, tires screeching. But she couldn't just leave him there.

Lindsay opened the door, mentally rehearsing every self-defense move she could remember from the women's safety videos she'd seen in high school. By now, though, she felt fairly sure she wouldn't need them. After all, this was Fred, and if one of them was crazy, it was probably her.

It was a strange feeling, being wedged into Lindsay's little metallic vehicle. His legs were bent far up in front of him, close to the front of the car. Still, he could find no room for complaint. She'd allowed him into her car, and that was progress.

Lindsay flicked a little switch on the console between them. "The heater takes a few minutes to warm up. Sorry."

"Not a problem." She had no way of knowing

how true that was. Cold was something he felt from the outside, something that made the air bracing and invigorating, but it didn't penetrate him. He had no idea how it would feel to *be* cold. He hadn't been above using Lindsay's perception of cold to his advantage, however, to get invited into her car.

Lindsay wasn't going to make his job easy, that was clear. But it would be enjoyable.

And sitting beside her while she drove made a fine opportunity to study her. Street lights came and went as they drove past, playing over her hair—a very fair shade of brown, nothing so simple as blond. He'd noticed the way it caught the light at the party tonight; even in this dimness, it did fascinating things. Her delicate features were contemplative, her knuckles just a little tense around the wheel. Well, no wonder. She was escorting someone who, not long ago, she'd considered a maniac. But she'd been kind enough to offer him a ride.

Not a cold person at all. In fact, for all her attempt at sharp edges, she seemed very vulnerable. What kept her closed off?

She gave him a sideways glance. "That seat adjusts, you know."

He frowned. "What do you mean?"

"I mean you don't have to ride with your knees in your mouth." She cast him another glance, and this time she smiled. Definite progress. "There's a

31

lever," she said. "At the bottom of the seat, on your right."

He groped under the seat until he found it. After some fumbling, the seat slid back. Not enough to let him straighten his legs fully, but it helped.

"Nice party," he commented. "Nice people."

"Thanks." The corner of her mouth curved up again, just a little. She refrained from reminding him he hadn't been invited.

"What do you do there? Phil talked about it, but I'm afraid I missed the gist."

"Corporate-investor relations. It's like public relations, only more boring." Another sideways smile. It warmed him in a way no car heater ever could. Fred thought he could bask in one of those smiles for a very long time.

Because it meant he was making progress on her case, of course.

"So," Lindsay said, fingering the steering wheel, "how did you like Phil's collection of ships in bottles?"

"I thought it was very interesting, actually. Although he told me he hasn't built a new one in over ten years. That seems a shame."

"That's why he's always so happy to meet someone who hasn't seen them yet."

"You like him, don't you?"

She nodded. She'd never given it much thought before, but not every pair of bosses would bring employees into their home for a Christmas party. Phil and Evelyn could be almost parental; they were quick to notice when someone wasn't getting enough sleep, or might have had a recent breakup. It could be a little oppressive at times, but they meant well.

"He's very fond of you," Fred said. "They all are."

Fond of what? she wondered. She'd felt so awkward tonight. Surrounded by all those familiar faces, outside the office, she hadn't known what to say to any of them.

"Jeanne's nice too," he said.

Lindsay's hands tightened on the wheel. This time there was no denying the irrational bug of jealousy—when she should be planning to warn Jeanne to keep her front door shut. Or giving Fred a lift directly to Bellevue, magical shirts or not. And booking a room there for herself while she was at it. In the opposite wing, as far away from the man as she could get.

"Watch out for Matthew, though. His intentions aren't honorable."

"What?" Her head snapped around. "Matt, the accountant? He *said* that?"

"He didn't have to. It's written all over his face, every time he looks at you. You never noticed?"

"No." It would take a while to get her mind to stop reeling from that one. Matt's whole conversation with her had consisted of a blow-by-blow description of his car's new sound system, all six or seven channels of it. Phil's ship-in-a-bottle collection would have been infinitely better.

"You know," Fred said, "we just spent an evening in a room full of people who like you very much. They just don't feel they know you very well. Why is that?"

"Never mind." Lindsay clutched the wheel again, then forced her fingers to relax. She slid a glance at Fred out of the corner of her eye. "Tell me more about Matt."

"Lindsay!" For one second he was every inch the proper Victorian. Then he saw her grin, and he laughed.

They both laughed. Together. It felt like a dangerous precedent. "I knew you had a sense of humor," he said.

When they had finished laughing, it got quiet in the car. Lindsay fixed her eyes on the street ahead, keenly aware that Fred was watching her.

He said, almost thoughtfully, "You're not seeing anyone, are you?"

It sounded more like a statement than a question. And maybe just a little too casual. Lindsay kept her hands relaxed on the wheel and tried to match his offhanded tone. "No one in particular. Why?"

"It just doesn't seem right to me, I suppose. Someone as lovely as you, unattached."

From anyone else, that would have sounded like a blatant pick-up line. But Fred didn't sound smarmy or flirty. He sounded, in fact, genuinely puzzled.

Lindsay shrugged, still feigning a casual attitude. "It's not like I never go out. There just isn't anyone serious right now."

"Odd. You seem like the serious type."

"And you're starting to seem like the nosy type." She smiled again to lighten the comeback.

It had the desired effect. Fred smiled back and dropped the subject.

They reached the hotel. Just in time, Lindsay told herself. She was starting to like him. Worse, if she were honest with herself, she'd liked him for quite a while.

The Broadway Hotel stood on Lakeside Boulevard, one of the main streets in town, now fully decked out for the holidays. Christmas lights stretched from one side of the street to the other, their red and green sparkling like the frosting on a Christmas cookie. She could tell why Fred had been drawn to the spot. She stopped in front of the hotel and waited for him to get out.

Obligingly, he reached for the door handle. "One more thing," he said. "I know I've been telling you to spare yourself all this holiday stress. But you were right about the fudge."

"What?"

"The fudge you bring in every year. Apparently it's not to be missed. Several people mentioned it to me. It wouldn't be Christmas without it, they said." He sounded approving.

"I told you so."

"Well, thank you for the ride. It was very nice of you." He opened the door, and Lindsay endured a blast of cold air as she watched Fred's long legs disentangle themselves from underneath the dashboard.

Lindsay waited until he was out of the car. Only then did she get up the nerve to ask him what she'd sensed underneath her skin all along, and somehow chosen to ignore. "Fred? You didn't really need a ride anywhere, did you?"

"I didn't need the *transportation*," he amended. "The ride was lovely. Good night, Lindsay."

If anyone had been looking at Fred Holliday at that particular moment, they would have seen a tall, dark man simply cease to exist, leaving an empty space on the sidewalk.

Of course, he knew enough to make sure no one saw. He certainly didn't want to give some poor innocent bystander a coronary for Christmas.

After the brightly colored street, reporting to Headquarters was a bit jarring. If this realm had a color, he supposed, it would be pure white, but there was nothing to see. Likewise, there was nothing to hear, yet he recognized his immediate supervisor's voice quite plainly.

I take it you're here to report on the Lindsay Miller case?

Yes. This isn't going to be easy, is it? It's taken the better part of two nights just to convince her that I exist.

That's typical.

She has some impressive barriers.

That's one of the reasons you were sent. Remember, this is all for her good.

If you really wanted results, you should have sent me in August. Is there any way I might be able to get more time?

Not unless you care to have us change the scheduling of a two-thousand-year-old holiday. There was no audible tone, yet the rebuff was plain. *You'll manage.*

He found himself reluctant to comment on Lindsay, beyond those generalities. It seemed— unfair to her, somehow.

His superior prompted him: *What do you plan to do next?*

He knew just the thing, but he didn't elaborate. *I think I'll play it by ear.*

Yes, that's probably your strongest skill. But before you go, I have some more pertinent information on her case. . . .

Chapter 3

When Fred showed up on her doorstep the next morning with a seven-foot fir tree, Lindsay didn't know why she was even surprised.

The day had begun with a call from Evelyn, before Lindsay got out of bed. It had snowed overnight, and the roads were closed, so the office would be closed today too. Lindsay suspected the roads would be open by late morning—they usually were—and also suspected Evelyn knew that. Snow was common in this part of Colorado, but it rarely stayed on the ground for more than a day or two. She had the feeling Evelyn welcomed the excuse to stay home and do some more Christmas preparations, as much as any of her employees.

Lindsay resolved not to waste any time. She'd just discovered eight extra hours, and she wanted to make the best use of them. Fudge for the office? Or get more of her Christmas cards ready to mail? The cards still sat stacked on the tray in front of the sofa, untouched since that memorable interruption the night before last. Lindsay's eyes went from the tray to the kitchen and back again.

Before she could decide on her task, the doorbell rang.

She opened the door, and there Fred stood on her snow-covered porch, holding a Christmas tree propped up beside him like a friend he was about to introduce. He'd returned to full Victorian regalia, long overcoat, ruffled shirt, top hat and all. Along with a jaunty red scarf she didn't remember from before.

Lindsay stared. "Some guys give flowers," she finally said.

He responded with—what else?—a hearty laugh. He turned the tree slowly on the base of its trunk for Lindsay's inspection, offering a view from all sides. "What do you think of it?"

It looked gorgeous, full and beautifully shaped, with no skimpy spots she could see. The incomparable scent of pine teased her nostrils. Lindsay resisted the urge to finger a branch and test the needles for freshness. "I'm sure it'll look lovely in your hotel room."

"That's not where it's needed." She noticed he neither confirmed nor denied having a room at the hotel. "There's a spot in front of your living room window that's just crying for a tree." He turned his head toward her front window, where her Christmas tree had stood every year until this one. And to think she'd bought the little artificial one to simplify matters.

Lindsay felt as if she stood at the threshold in more ways than one. If she let him in now, she might never get rid of him. But how did you close the door on a man who brought you a whole tree?

You said "no thank you" and closed the door. Maybe he'd finally get the hint. Or maybe he'd just appear on the other side of her door again, tree and all.

She tried anyway. "Fred, I told you, I already have a tree."

"No, you have a little artificial electric weed." His dark eyes teased and coaxed her at the same time. "Come on, now. You know what a difference it will make."

If she closed the door now, she'd feel like the original Scrooge. "I had plans this morning—"

"Your plan was to go to work. That's been cancelled. You have a few hours of extra time. It's a gift. It shouldn't be thrown away."

She had cards to mail, and fudge to make.

She had a man standing in front of her with a full-size, fragrant tree, and the most beguiling smile she'd ever seen. Someone who'd shown her nothing but warmth, even if he did have trouble taking no for an answer.

For the first time, she admitted to herself that she wasn't so sure she *wanted* him to go away.

Lindsay looked at the spot in front of her window, vacant except for a potted plant, easily moved. And she pulled the door open and stepped aside.

"Wonderful." Fred swept in past her, bringing the breath of fresh pine into her apartment. Belatedly, she thought to wonder where he'd gotten a tree this time of morning, with all of the roads closed.

Before she closed the door, she looked out on her porch. Pristine snow surrounded it in all directions, except for some impressions where Fred and the tree had just been standing.

No footprints leading up to it. No trail of needles. Just smooth, white snow.

Lindsay shivered.

"Here, now, before you catch your death." Fred's hand came to rest lightly on her arm, pulling her gently back to close the door. She'd shivered, but it hadn't been from the wintry draft.

Fred propped the tree against the wall with care and started to take off his jacket, as if to get down to business. "Oh, I almost forgot." He put a hand in his pocket and withdrew a sprig of mistletoe, tied with a red velvet bow. He reached up easily and tied it to the hanging lamp over her apartment's small entryway. "No home should be without it for the holidays."

Lindsay edged back, out from underneath the lamp, but if Fred noticed her discomfiture, he didn't show it. He pulled off his coat and draped it neatly over the back of her couch with a smile. "I assume you have a Christmas tree stand?"

Lindsay nodded weakly and went to the hall closet, making a wide circle of the mistletoe.

What have I done?

What she had done, she found, was to let in an inexhaustible source of Christmas cheer.

Within half an hour, the tree was installed in its stand, Christmas carols were playing on her stereo, and Fred was trying to master the inevitably tangled lights. She'd seen a number of men wrestle with Christmas lights, but until now, she'd never seen one do it without swearing. "Electrical things aren't my strong suit," was his only comment.

Not comfortable with electrical things. And he didn't drive. So many little peculiarities, and so many seeming impossibilities. Last night she'd accepted it without much question, mostly out of dumb shock. Today Lindsay found herself grasping for explanations. Where had he *really* come from?

"White Christmas" drifted to Lindsay from the stereo, and she thought of an experiment. "Name the singer," she said casually. Playfully.

He didn't miss a beat. "Bing Crosby. Everyone knows that."

So he hadn't walked directly out of the nineteenth century. He was familiar with things that dated, at least, from the 1930s or '40s. About the time of the movie she'd been watching. That didn't help much at all.

Lindsay's temples started to throb with the warnings of another headache. A headache that felt out of place with "O Come All Ye Faithful" in the background. She'd be better off putting her questions aside for now, she decided.

Her headache faded.

She and Fred started winding the lights around the tree, standing on opposite sides so they could pass the lighted string back and forth between them. "I like these," Fred said, fingering one of the bulbs as he handed the strand to her again. "Most people these days seem to prefer the tiny little bulbs."

Lindsay considered her larger, multicolored lights. "This is the size we always had on my tree at home when I was growing up."

"I'm letting you off easy, you know. A proper tree should have tinsel as well."

"Let me guess." She peered around the branches at him. "One strand at a time?"

"Absolutely." He grinned. "Although I admit, that may not be the best thing for your personality type. You make things complex enough as it is."

The grin hit her just as his fingertips brushed hers to hand her the lights again. Lindsay ducked back behind the branches to hide the blush that started in her cheeks, spread to her ears, and quickly made it all the way down to her toes.

"Who's Steven?"

Lindsay's head jerked up, but the branches between them obscured Fred's face. Her heart thrummed in her ears. Then she remembered a fortune-teller's trick she'd heard about: firing off a random question, in the hope of making a direct hit.

Lindsay said, "I have a cousin named Steven."

"No, not that one." Any self-respecting quack fortune-teller, Lindsay suspected, would have seized the bait. "This would be someone more significant."

"You tell me." Still holding her end of the lights, Lindsay stepped to one side of the tree and leveled her eyes at Fred with as much of a poker face as she could muster. Her mouth felt dry, but she kept her voice even. "Either you know who he is or you don't."

"No, my information from Headquarters is strictly on a need-to-know basis. The rest is for you to tell me. They've only told me that you and Steven are to be reconciled."

Suddenly, she didn't care *where* he came from.

She just wanted him to go back there. Lindsay dropped her end of the lights. "That's it."

Fred caught the lights. "What?"

That guileless stare of his again. Lindsay felt the hot sting of betrayal. To think she'd actually let him into her home. "This is some kind of game. You've been spying on me. Or else someone must have—"

"Now, see here." The sudden firmness in his voice surprised her. "I've had about all of this I can take."

"*You've* had all—"

"Yes."

The Christmas lights in his hands flared to twice their brightness, then blinked out.

He didn't seem to notice. "I understand this can be hard to accept at first, and I've been patient. I bring a tree to your door, and at least you're ready to accept that. But the minute I bring you a bit of news that's not to your liking, you're ready to shoot the messenger. Is that fair?" He didn't raise his voice, but his mouth was drawn in a firm line that looked out of place on his features.

Her eyes went down to the darkened lights in his hands. An electrical surge, she tried to tell herself. Sure. And somehow he'd managed to rearrange the snow on her walkway before he knocked on her door. She'd hallucinated the carols on the phone. And of course, it was pure coincidence that made this man a dead ringer for the actor she'd been watching on television moments before Fred appeared in her life.

When she raised her eyes to his face, he locked her in a steady gaze. He didn't look like he was playing a game. He looked genuinely offended. "What proof do you need that I'm telling you the truth?"

She looked down again at the lights.

Up again at his eyes, still fixed on hers.

And swallowed hard.

"Steven was my boyfriend in high school," she said. "I haven't seen him in years."

He frowned. But this time, seemingly, not at her. "That's odd. I wouldn't have thought of match-making as my strong suit." His frown deepened. "What was he, some sort of beast?"

No, she thought, *I was.*

"No," he mused, "that can't be it. That wouldn't be in your best interest, and that's what this is all about." The lines between his brows faded. "Still, I suppose there's no law saying that's the *first* thing we have to deal with."

The string of lights came back on. But he wasn't looking at the lights. He was looking at her.

Fred held the strand out to Lindsay, ready to continue their work. As far as she could tell, he'd never noticed they'd gone out.

Lindsay stared at the lights, then at Fred. "This isn't normal."

Fred met her eyes as he put the bright string of bulbs into her hand. "Now you're beginning to get it," he said softly.

Lindsay tried to concentrate on stringing the lights. Or the prickling of the pine needles. National disasters. Anything was better than the unwelcome thoughts now crowding her brain.

Why did Fred have to bring up Steven? And how could he and "Headquarters" know about Steven . . . unless Fred was exactly what he said he was?

Just when she thought this situation couldn't get any stranger, now he was bringing her old boyfriend into it. She hadn't seen Steven in ten years. Hadn't thought about him in . . . well, that was a lie. He was there in the shadows, especially this time of year. Because they'd broken up this time of year, and it had ended so badly.

Didn't Headquarters know anything about letting sleeping dogs lie? Some doors were better left closed, and she was pretty sure Steven would agree with her.

She sneaked a peek at Fred through the pine branches. It would make so much more sense if he'd appeared as a reproachful, chain-rattling Jacob Marley. He claimed to be her personal spirit of Christmas Present, so why was he dredging up the past?

It didn't make sense, but it was getting harder all the time to deny that this was real.

She knew Fred was watching her, trying to read her expression, even though every time she glanced at him he, too, appeared focused on the Christmas tree. With the effort they were putting into hanging these lights, the tree ought to be a masterpiece by the time they were done.

Fred let the Christmas carols from the stereo fill the silence while they finished with the lights. Lindsay's disquieted features, and her slightly unfocused expression, let him know she had some thinking to do. Best not to interrupt. Besides, he needed to do some thinking of his own.

What in the world could Headquarters be thinking?

Why send *him* to play matchmaker between a beautiful woman and her ex-boyfriend? If he'd known, he certainly wouldn't have brought the mistletoe. He'd meant it as more or less a joke, although he wouldn't have been above stealing a kiss if the opportunity presented itself. All in the spirit of holiday cheer, of course.

The box of ornaments from Lindsay's closet brought a much-needed change of mood. As soon as she knelt on the floor and parted the cardboard flaps, he saw it in her face. The soft light of rediscovery.

She'd liked the tree. She liked the Christmas carols, or she wouldn't have over fifty discs of them. But this box contained things much closer to Lindsay's heart. He knelt across from her to get a better look. Not at the contents of the box, but at the expressions that crossed her face as memories flooded in.

"My first nutcracker." She volunteered the information unprompted. "One of the first decorations I bought with my own money. And here's one of the crystal ballerinas . . ."

A haphazard inventory began as Lindsay unwrapped the ornaments from napkins and tissues and laid them out on the floor. All of the ornaments were different—from different decades, and probably, at various times, different households. No sterile, color-coordinated ornaments, aside from the occasional bright-colored ball to be used as filler. This would be a tree filled with sentiment, and Fred realized he hadn't expected anything less of her.

After a few minutes she handed him a toy soldier, and stood to hang the first of her ballerinas. As they worked, Fred took care to let Lindsay gravitate toward her favorites, sometimes with a comment or a story, sometimes not. Then he spotted one that had the unmistakable air of a treasured memento.

"Now, here's something you don't see every day." He held up a bedraggled reindeer stick horse, with a huge Styrofoam head and a fake candy cane for a body.

"Oh, let me hang that one." Lindsay snatched it from his fingers and hung it low on the tree, but near the center, where it wouldn't be missed.

"That's Rudolph. My mom let me take him when I moved away from home." She fingered the reindeer's bent green tinfoil antlers. "When I was little I always used to hang him from some nice high branch. Then I'd wonder why he turned up in a lower spot later on. Usually near the back." She put her hands in front of her face to hide her smile. "Isn't he hideous?"

"Some of the best Christmas decorations are hideous." Fred peered into the light gray eyes above her folded hands. Undeniably, they sparkled.

And you were going to leave these boxed up in the closet all year?

He refrained from saying it.

The tree filled quickly. Soon there was very little space left, even for those generic ball ornaments, most of which went at the back of the tree. A smattering of decorations still covered the bottom of the box when Lindsay closed the cardboard flaps with a reluctant last look. "I guess I'll have to save these for next year."

Next year. He liked the sound of that.

Fred flicked out the switch for the overhead living room light, and they both stood back to admire their handiwork. The gray wintry day outside left the apartment fairly dim, so the tree's colorful lights had a chance to do their work, transforming the room into a picture of holiday tranquility.

Lindsay stood in the soft light with her arms wrapped around herself. "Thanks," she said, meeting his eyes. A smile touched her lips, and tugged at his heart. It was her most unreserved moment to date.

And if he let it continue, he might forget himself and put his arm around her, whether her case called for it or not. *Remember the job.*

In the glow of the Christmas tree, that was hard to do. Fred stepped back to the light switch and turned it on. It bought him the distance he needed, but at the cost of the peaceful mood they'd just managed to capture. One glance at Lindsay confirmed he'd broken the moment. She surveyed the boxes they'd emptied, as though calculating the effort it would take to fit them back into the closet.

"So," he said, "what's next?" He winced. His tone sounded overly bright, even to him. Not good.

Lindsay twisted her fingers in her hair. Fred could see the demons returning. Time to pull her shell back around herself. Why did she keep herself boxed away, like those ornaments that now decorated her tree?

"Cards and fudge," she said.

"Oh, yes, the cards." Fred wandered to the little wooden tray, heaped with cards and bright green envelopes, and glanced at her open address book. "That's quite a stack. And you're only on the *G's*?"

"Do you mind?"

"Excuse me, I didn't mean to pry." He stepped back. "Hazard of my profession. Who are all these people, anyway?"

He could absolutely feel some tiny coil inside her tighten. "My family. Friends from high school, and college . . ."

"Why don't you just send them all postcards and be done with it?"

"This is the only time of year most of them hear from me."

He quirked a brow at her. *And why is that?* "What about a newsletter, then?"

"Too impersonal. Anyway, single people don't do newsletters. That's for people with kids who play soccer and take piano lessons."

Fred noticed that while she was defending to the death the need to write the cards, she hadn't taken a single step toward the tray. He smiled at her gently. "Lindsay, you hate these cards."

She blinked at the word. "I don't *hate* them."

"Well, they're the bane of your existence, then." This time she didn't argue. "I could at least address the envelopes for you."

"It has to be in my—"

"—own handwriting." He nodded gravely as he finished along with her. "I should have known. Has it ever occurred to you that you make things harder than they need to be? Why not call your friends during the year?"

Her fingers still wound through her hair. Sometimes she seemed like a ball of consternation, a tangle of knots he yearned to unravel. But many of his ideas for doing so, he felt sure, wouldn't pass muster at Headquarters. And they probably wouldn't be too popular with this Steven, either. Not if the man had any sense.

"All right, then," he said. "I can help you with the fudge."

Her hand dropped from her hair. "You've got to be kidding."

"No, let's look at this. How much fudge do you need to make?"

"Two batches. One with almonds and one without. And it's a complicated recipe. You couldn't—"

"Oh? Care to make a bet on that?"

"You *are* kidding."

"No. Here's the deal." This was much better. Perversely, he found it far easier to deal with her arguments than with her vulnerability. One sharpened his wits. The other one seemed bent on making him forget why he was here. "How long does it take you to make one batch of fudge?"

She bit her lip. "About forty-five minutes."

"Do you have two pots?"

"Yes. But there's no way—"

"Wait. You haven't heard my terms yet." Fred folded his arms, leaning back against the wall next to the light switch. "I'm a quick study. You make a batch, I make a batch. I'll do exactly what you do." She opened her mouth to object again. He held up a hand. "If we don't turn out two perfect batches of fudge in the time it would have taken you to make one—I leave you alone."

Her mouth stayed open. Did the thought of having him go away still appeal to her? He hoped not. But he pressed forward.

"If I lose, I'll leave you in peace. No arguments." He paused, then played his trump card. "No Steven."

She flinched at the name. What kind of person *was* this man?

"However. If I win." He drew in a deep breath. "You agree to let me take you on a proper Christmas adventure tomorrow night. Again, no arguments."

He studied Lindsay's face. So much went on

behind those eyes. Strangely, the longer he knew her, the less sure he felt of what those thoughts might be.

Finally her mouth turned up in another smile. "Okay. On one condition."

He straightened from the wall. "What's that?"

"If you ruin a batch of fudge, you have to replace all the chocolate and marshmallows we waste."

"*Sixteen* marshmallows," Fred repeated. "Not fifteen. Not seventeen . . ."

Lindsay rested one hand on her hip while the other hand stirred in the marshmallows she'd just added to her saucepan. "Remember. The deal is, you do it my way."

"Oh, I'm not arguing. I just wonder what bizarre chemical reaction might happen if—"

"Hush." The sparkle had returned to her eyes, and the cloud of stress had faded as they stood side by side in front of her stove, assembling the ingredients. In her kitchen, all uncertainty dissolved, and Lindsay transformed into a woman in control. Fred was no fool. He added in his marshmallows.

"Where did you get this recipe, anyway? Your grandmother?"

Lindsay blushed. "Internet."

"You can't be serious." He raised his eyebrows.

"I've heard of people using computers for other things, like meeting someone to marry. But something as important as fudge?"

"Well, sort of. I started out with a bunch of recipes I found on the Internet. Then I experimented. I like to add some milk chocolate in with the semisweet. And a lot of people use marshmallow creme in a jar, but I—"

"I bow to your expertise. Just show me how it's done."

Lindsay continued stirring, with Fred following her example. A thoughtful crease appeared across her brow as she bent over her task. Her hair slipped forward to partially obscure her face like a curtain, falling in waves of whisper-light brown. It looked unbearably soft. He felt an irrational urge to bury his fingers in it.

"You've never used a computer, have you?" Her question caught him off guard.

"Never needed to. I'm more of a field staffer."

"Do they use computers, where you come from?"

Too many questions, and about things that didn't matter. "The mix is boiling," he said. "What now?"

"It never comes to a boil this fast." Lindsay's attention shifted to the critical matter at hand. "Quick, keep stirring. I forgot the candy thermometer." Still stirring her own pot, she took a wide step to her left with one foot and rummaged in a drawer just barely within her reach. Her eyes widened in alarm. "I didn't think. I only have one candy thermometer."

"So we'll time my batch to match yours. What's the worst that can happen? You'll still have one good batch of fudge, and I'll be out of your way."

She might have looked displeased at the thought, even as she scrabbled through the kitchen drawer. He hoped so. But if she hadn't sensed from the beginning how heavily this bet was hedged, she still had a lot to learn about him.

Lindsay retrieved the candy thermometer and clipped it inside her saucepan. For a few minutes they stirred side by side in silence. Now and then she hunkered down, knees bent so she was at eye level with the candy thermometer, watching for that crucial temperature, as intent as any emergency-room physician. For Lindsay, fudge was serious business. But it didn't seem to bear the burdensome weight of those awful cards in the living room.

"You enjoy this, don't you?" he said.

"I guess so. It gets exhausting after a while, though. By the end of last week I felt like my arm was going to fall off from all the stirring. But it's something I'm good at."

"And that's important?"

She flashed him a menacing look. "Menace"

being a relative term, coming from someone nearly a foot shorter than he was. "Keep stirring."

"So amateur psychology isn't one of my strong suits. We'll add it to the list, along with electrical things and computers."

Lindsay didn't seem to hear him. She was peering at the candy thermometer again. The sheer depth of her concentration put a strange little ache in his chest.

You know, you could probably use that computer network of yours to find Steven, too. Provided that finding him was the problem. But he wasn't about to upset the applecart by tossing that name out again. He wasn't anxious to think of it himself.

Steven should be pounding this woman's door down, not the other way around. If they'd sent Fred to work the other end of the case and help Steven reconcile with Lindsay, it would have been much easier. He could have shoved Steven at some unknown pretty girl with both hands, before he had a chance to know her.

But Lindsay must need him for something else, or he wouldn't be here. So he'd bring Christmas to her the best way he knew how: one moment at a time.

Finally Lindsay pronounced the mixture hot enough to add the chocolate chips. Followed by yet more stirring, until at last she determined it was time to remove it from the heat.

"All right," he said. "Ready for the moment of truth?"

Lindsay looked at him quizzically.

Fred held a wooden spoonful of fudge up in front of her, waving it lightly through the air to cool it. "Here. Time to see if I've got it right."

Lindsay looked at him over the spoon, a wonderful complication of emotions in her eyes. Did she want him to win or lose the bet? Fred wasn't sure she knew the answer herself. She turned her face up toward him as he held the spoon to her lips. And then, as she tasted it, she closed her eyes, savoring the chocolate. Her expression was one of blissful surrender.

This was the real Lindsay, her face unguarded, completely in the moment. Very much like a woman lost in a kiss.

He never should have brought the bloody mistletoe.

Chapter 4

Dear Aunt Arline,
    Hope this finds you feeling well. How's the
weather in Minnesota?
    It's a little late in the season, but this morning
I put up my Christmas tree with

Lindsay scratched out the word "with" and put a period at the end of the sentence. There was no way she could explain Fred.

The carols on the stereo had stopped. Out of sheer stubbornness, Lindsay tried to keep working, but the silence nagged at her. Finally she got up. But before she changed the music, she went into the kitchen for some eggnog. Only because it would expire soon.

Okay, so Fred was right about some things. He hadn't really been telling her anything she didn't already know. For years, she'd been trying to get more out of Christmas. That was why she bought eggnog in the first place.

But Steven?

Fred was way off base on that one. His "Headquarters" database must have a huge glitch. After the way she'd left things with Steven, the man would probably throw rocks at her if he ever saw her again. It hadn't been the right way to break up with a boyfriend; it wasn't even a good way to treat a friend. And Steven *had* been a friend, her best friend, all through high school.

Their dating relationship came so gradually that Lindsay was hard-pressed to remember exactly when it started. They'd met the summer before their freshman year in high school, when Steven moved into Lindsay's neighborhood. He lived a block away, so there was no need for a car when they started getting together to study. Lindsay was horrible at algebra; Steven never knew where to put a comma in an essay. It was a seamless give-and-take.

When there were dances at school, they paired up. No need to wait around, hoping some guy she barely knew would ask her. Not even that good-looking football player, who ended up getting expelled for sneaking booze into one too many school events. So wasn't it just as well?

She did remember their first kiss, a nose-bumping affair outside Lindsay's front door, and that she was glad it was Steven because neither of them had to be embarrassed about it. What she didn't remember was any spark. Nothing like the way she'd felt when Fred's hand brushed hers just handing her the Christmas tree lights.

Steven had liked Christmas too. And Lindsay had loved it. There'd been so much more time for things then—no obligations other than school and, later, a part-time job at McDonald's. Not nearly so many people to buy for. Plenty of time for planning and wrapping and finding just the right present. Steven had been easy to shop for; they were together so much she knew exactly what kind of sweater he needed or what CD he wanted. Everything had come so naturally.

But in all that time, she couldn't remember hours disappearing as fast as they just had with Fred.

Crazy talk. Fred wasn't here to date her, and the sooner he was out of her life, the better. Maybe following through with things like carols and eggnog would fulfill enough of his mission for him to go away, and he wouldn't even show up tomorrow night.

She told herself that was what she wanted.

Returning to the living room, she put on the hokiest country Christmas music CD she could find. It sounded like just the thing to send any self-respecting Englishman running for the hills.

It wasn't so easy to dispel him from her thoughts.

Getting ready for work the next morning, Lindsay reached into her closet, and somewhat to her surprise, came out with her brightest red sweater. She pulled it on and studied the reflection in her bathroom mirror with a critical eye. The vivid red fit the season, but it washed out the color of her hair, a bland shade that was neither blond nor brown. To compensate, she spent some extra time on her makeup, bringing a touch more color to her cheeks and eyes. It helped. But something was missing. The next thing she knew, she was hunting through her jewelry box for her old pair of dime-store candy cane earrings.

She ended up late for work, but no one seemed to mind once they saw she'd brought two plates of fudge.

"So how's your merry gentleman?"

Jeanne sauntered into Lindsay's little cubicle of an office and perched on the corner of her desk, a square of fudge in hand.

Lindsay couldn't help smiling. She had to admit it was a good description of Fred. "He's fine. Helped me out with the fudge, as a matter of fact."

"It's extra good this year. Not that it isn't always. But you know what I mean."

Lindsay knew, all right. The fudge had been

disappearing fast all morning—particularly the batch Fred had made, although the fudge with almonds usually went more slowly.

Jeanne lazily swung one leg up and down. If any man had been in the room, Lindsay knew he wouldn't be able to take his eyes off that unconscious, coquettish swing of her calf. "I can't believe you never mentioned him," she said. "Where'd he come from?"

How to answer that? England, over a hundred years ago. Or out of her television screen. She certainly couldn't talk about "Headquarters," whatever that was. "A friend of a friend. He's just visiting for a little while."

"Maybe he'll like it here." A playful glimmer appeared in Jeanne's blue eyes. "He sure seemed to like you." She polished off her last bite of fudge. Almond, Lindsay noted, before it disappeared into Jeanne's mouth. "He was asking all about you. Then, next thing I knew, I was telling him all about my cats." She rolled her eyes. "The funny thing is, he acted like he was actually listening."

Lindsay thought of Phil and his model ships. "He's good at that. Listening, that is."

"Sounds like a keeper to me." Jeanne stopped swinging one long, slender leg, and started with the other. Matt passed by and almost walked into the wall of the next cubicle as he turned to look.

Lindsay wondered if Fred had noticed Matt's intentions toward Jeanne, too.

Oblivious to the broken nose she'd nearly caused, Jeanne went on. "If you got married, would that make him a U.S. citizen?"

Lindsay felt her face grow hot. "I doubt it." Jeanne always seemed to be in a hurry to see a relationship turn serious. Little did she know how unlikely it was in this case. It would be pretty hard, after all, to go into a commitment with a man who could appear and disappear at will.

Now was a good time to change the subject. Lindsay asked, "How's it going with you and Brad?"

"Same old, same old. I'm waiting to see if he starts a fight before Christmas the way he did right before my birthday. I swear some guys plan that stuff, just so they don't have to shop for a present." She boosted herself off Lindsay's desk. "Well, I better get back to work. Want to do lunch at the Thai place today?"

Lindsay hesitated. The Thai restaurant two blocks away was an occasional treat for her and Jeanne, a chance to eat the kind of "girl food" no man they dated ever wanted to try. What did men know of coconut soup and Thai iced coffee?

In fact, Jeanne had introduced Lindsay to the food herself, the second week Lindsay worked here. The pretty blonde had known just what the stressed-out new girl needed while she struggled to adjust to her first full-time job. Jeanne had been reassuring and supportive, and Lindsay had been surprised to find how much she had in common with someone who was so outwardly different.

A Thai lunch was tempting, but . . . "I've got Christmas cards to do." She'd brought along a plastic grocery sack full of them, to work on during lunch. She'd barely gotten past the letter *M* yesterday. There were a lot of Millers in her family.

"Oh, come on. It might be our last chance before you go on vacation."

Jeanne's tone held an imploring note. Maybe she was right. Lindsay was taking the week off between Christmas and New Year's to visit her parents, so they were running out of work days. Plus, Lindsay remembered Jeanne saying that Brad's idea of "out to dinner" rarely involved anything beyond ground beef in a bun. Not the most accommodating of males.

And after all, what were friends for? "Okay."

Jeanne beamed and sashayed out the door.

Later that morning, Lindsay paused as she walked by the fudge on the long table in the middle of the office, next to the coffee machine. After making eleven batches of fudge last week—which, naturally, had to be sampled for quality—she didn't quite have her usual appetite for chocolate. But she picked up a piece of Fred's batch with the almonds and took a bite. Sure enough, it tasted nearly as knee-bucklingly good as it had in her kitchen yesterday, when the fudge was still warm.

Lindsay nipped a tiny corner off a piece of her fudge and took a quick taste. His *was* better than hers. But how? He'd stood right next to her, done exactly what she did.

She took one extra piece of the almond fudge back to her desk to save for later, before it all ran out. She was glad she did. By the time she and Jeanne returned from lunch, both of the plates she'd brought were empty.

Through the rest of the afternoon, the little square of fudge teased her from its hiding place, safely tucked in a coffee filter at the far corner of her desk. She made herself wait, forcing herself to focus on the stack of client statements that had to be done before she went on vacation. As the day stretched on, Lindsay tried not to glance at her old Timex watch any more than usual. Whatever Fred had in store for tonight, she'd find out soon enough.

She told herself that. But it didn't keep her mind from conjuring up the image of laughing dark eyes, filled with some secret promise. Lindsay tried not to think about it, the same way she tried to ignore that hidden square of fudge. No. Not until she'd gotten enough work done.

At four-twenty-five, she finally decided she'd earned it. Lindsay went to the coffee machine and poured half a cup of late-afternoon brew to go with her chocolate. On her way back to her desk, she heard a deep, resonant laugh from inside her cubicle.

Lindsay turned the corner, and there stood Fred, lounging against the filing cabinet beside her desk, eating her last piece of fudge, and chatting with her friend Jeanne.

He was hatless once again, his dark hair slightly tousled as though he'd just been walking outside, and Lindsay wondered distractedly if he ever really needed to walk anywhere. He wore the same overcoat and bright red scarf he'd worn yesterday morning, and his face exuded friendly cheer as he smiled at Jeanne. Lindsay's heart did a flip of its own accord; she'd been seeing him all afternoon, but her mind's eye hadn't done him justice. Hard to believe he was here because she'd *lost* a bet.

No, no, no. Two days ago you thought he was a figment of your imagination.

A gorgeous figment.

"He wouldn't dare," Fred said to Jeanne. Utter disbelief shimmered in his eyes. "If he starts a row with you before December twenty-fourth, you let me know. I'll have a word with him."

His glance went to the doorway, where Lindsay stood. And stayed there. His smile didn't widen; it deepened, with undisguised pleasure at seeing her.

He straightened from his half-leaning posture. "Lindsay."

Even her name sounded unusually beautiful to her. How was she supposed to act rational around a man like that?

Lindsay's eyes went to the last fragment of fudge in his hand. "That was my last piece." If it were anyone else, she would have wondered how he found it.

"Your last piece? It's my first." He blinked in wounded innocence. "You made me leave before it was ready to eat. Wait four hours to let it cool? Sadistic." He popped the small remainder of the fudge into his mouth.

Jeanne stared at her. "He helped you make it? And you didn't let him have *any*?"

Great. Now she was a Christmas-hating, fudge-hoarding hag. "I had cards to do."

"I offered to help with the cards. But no matter." Fred tossed the crumpled, empty coffee filter into her trash basket and turned that encompassing gaze on her once more. "I like your earrings."

The little candy canes. No one else had noticed; she'd almost forgotten about them.

"I know I'm a little early," he said. "I thought it would be best to get a good head start."

"I can't leave early, I came in late—"

"Phil said it was all right."

He'd cleared it with Phil? Lindsay glanced at

Jeanne, whose raised eyebrows mirrored her own, then back at Fred. "You could sell ashes to the devil, couldn't you?"

"Maybe," he said lightly. "But why would I want to?" Jeanne laughed, but Lindsay wasn't sure whether or not it was a joke.

"Well, I'll let you two get going." Jeanne edged out of the room with a knowing smile. "Have fun."

These little blue-walled cubicles had never been roomy, but now, alone with Fred, the space seemed especially tight. Lindsay felt unaccountably shy, and far too aware that just a few feet separated them. They'd spent hours alone in her apartment yesterday, where they hadn't had an office full of people just a tottering partition away, but this felt different. More confining, maybe, and something about that seemed to pull her toward him.

Lindsay searched for somewhere else to look, and her eyes fell on the calendar on the wall next to her. December nineteenth. Only six more days to get everything done.

"You have reminders of time everywhere, don't you?" Fred moved toward her. "You're always worried about what's ahead. What you need to concentrate on is *now*. Otherwise you'll miss it." He reached into his overcoat pocket. "Here. You'll want this, where we're going."

Fred pulled out another scarf, this one red and white, and draped it lightly over her shoulders.

He drew her hair out from under the scarf, the warmth of his fingers lightly brushing the back of her neck. Lindsay fought back a pleasant shudder.

Fred's fingers lingered in her hair before he let it fall back into place, his expression unusually serious. His face was close to hers as he went through the motions of straightening the scarf, his eyes never leaving hers. What did he see there, and what was he thinking? She forced herself to breathe slowly, deeply, afraid to move, afraid he'd know what *she* was thinking. All she had to do was tilt her head back a little to raise her mouth toward his—

—and make a complete fool of herself.

Instead, Lindsay lowered her eyes to study the scarf—a more delicate knit than Fred's, made from yarn so soft it threatened to melt between her fingers. It was white with slim red stripes.

It matched the candy cane earrings.

"Thank you." Breaking the silence seemed to break the spell.

"It suits you." Fred stood back to give her another moment's contemplation, then smiled his approval. "Ready to go?"

"Maybe we should ask Jeanne to go with us." What? The words came out of her mouth unbidden. But something told her it might be smart not to spend too much time alone with Fred.

He appeared to consider it. "No, let's keep it

between the two of us tonight. We have a lot of ground to cover."

Half an hour later, Lindsay found herself riding beside Fred in a one-horse open sleigh.

Well, all right, a horse and carriage. But the bells on the horses' bridles jingled just like the ones in the song. White drifts of snow surrounded them on both sides of the road, piled high from the work of the snowplow yesterday. The lake district, just twenty minutes from Lindsay's home, got a lot more snow than her neighborhood, thanks to its higher altitude. And unlike the snow in her neighborhood, this snow would stay on the ground all winter long.

Lindsay looked back over her shoulder to make sure the street full of cars still existed behind them. It did. But the city had cordoned off two blocks for the Christmas street festival, so that it was only open to foot traffic and the horse-drawn carriages. The little shops and businesses in this area all sat shoulder to shoulder, sharing one long overhang that ran the length of the block. Long swags of small white Christmas lights hung from store to store. Street lamps, installed ten years ago but designed to look like their old gas-powered cousins, were wound with evergreen garland and red ribbon. Most of the downtown businesses closed by early evening, but out in front of the stores, pushcarts stood loaded down with wares that Lindsay strained for a better peek at as they passed. Pedestrians bustled purposefully or strolled casually among the carts, well bundled against the cold.

Up in the carriage, it was even colder, above the sidewalk with no protection from the wind. The frosty air bit her cheeks, and she pulled the big, heavy woven lap robe up around her.

She felt Fred's arm behind her, offering a little extra warmth. From any other man, the move would have seemed opportunistic. From Fred, she wasn't so sure. At this particular moment, Lindsay thought she might trust Fred more than she trusted herself. But sitting forward felt prim and uncomfortable as well as cold, so at last she gave in and settled back.

Sure enough, with Fred's firm, solid arm behind her shoulders, a sensation of warmth welcomed her. His coat sleeve held a woolen, masculine scent, and Lindsay held back a sigh. The inviting comfort of Fred beside her felt safe and dangerous at the same time.

"How did you know about this?" she asked.

"They do it every year, the week before Christmas. Didn't you know?"

"I've heard about it. But how did *you* know?"

"When it comes to Christmas, I make it my business to know. I suppose you've never been?"

"No." Lindsay saw his mouth tighten slightly, as though he were biting the inside of his lip to keep from saying something obvious. It was a look she was coming to recognize. "Go ahead," she challenged him. "Lecture me."

"Who learns anything from a lecture?" The carriage stopped. Fred climbed down ahead of her, then stood at the curb below, offering a hand up to her.

He hadn't worn the top hat tonight, but he didn't need it. With his charcoal black overcoat and bright red scarf, illuminated by the old-fashioned street lamps, he fit perfectly into the bustling holiday scene behind him. The hand he held out to her was bare. Lindsay hadn't thought to wear gloves; she suspected Fred didn't need them.

Sure enough, his hand was warm when she put hers into it. As she stepped down to join him, a blend of harmonized voices reached her ears.

Christmas is coming, the geese are getting fat
Please put a penny in the old man's hat.

Lindsay glanced down the sidewalk to the left. Carolers, in full Victorian costume. None of them looking as authentic as Fred did, even without his ruffled shirt and top hat.

If you haven't got a penny then a ha'penny will do
If you haven't got a ha'penny, then God bless you.

Fred kept Lindsay's hand in his to steady her until her feet made solid contact with the sidewalk below. It had to be close to freezing, so patches of ice were a distinct possibility. But the concrete under Lindsay's feet was gritty and solid. She felt an annoying pang of disappointment when he let go of her hand, but his smile still held her fast, even as the winter chill stung her cheeks once again. People shuffled around them; Lindsay moved closer to Fred to let them pass.

"Which way?" he asked her.

At a loss, Lindsay looked around. The carolers had stopped, to a smattering of applause, and Lindsay heard the clink of coins as they collected change in a tin cup. A pleasant confusion of aromas wrapped around her senses: the sweet smell of baked treats, tinged with the always-enticing scent of chocolate; hints of meat, bread, and spiced apple cider; and one very familiar scent that Lindsay couldn't quite identify. Smoky, sweet, slightly acrid . . . it niggled at her memory but wouldn't let go.

"What's that smell?" she asked, as if he could possibly know which one she meant. A wooden cart loaded with pastries threatened to roll over her toes, and Lindsay stepped back, this time closer to the window of a closed shoe store.

"Don't tell me you've never had roasted chestnuts."

"*That's* what it is!" She giggled. "I tried to cook them once."

The corners of his mouth quirked up. "And?"

"It . . . didn't work out."

Fred's mouth widened the rest of the way, into another of his ready smiles. "What went wrong?"

"I guess I should have found out *how* to cook them first. I figured, how hard can it be?" Lindsay stepped aside for a toddler swathed in a fat blue coat, closely pursued by a protective mother. "So I just popped them in my oven, a couple at a time, to see what worked. Nothing did. After a few minutes they'd explode. Sometimes they were dried up, sometimes they were smushy, but they all looked like monkeys' brains."

Fred laughed. "Well, then, you don't know what you're missing." He took her gently by the elbow— a habit she had to admit she was beginning not to mind—and steered her to the right. "Let's find out what you think of the real thing."

He guided her unerringly toward one of the street's many pushcarts. Clearly, it was the right one; the closer they got, the stronger the scent grew. "You do a lot of cooking, don't you?" he said.

"Not exactly. Baking, mostly. Cakes, cookies, fudge . . . then I'll heat up a frozen dinner. I've never learned to cook anything that's good for me."

"That makes us even. I never eat anything that's good for me." They reached the vendor, a short, swarthy man who probably would have been freezing if it weren't for the chestnut smoke. "Two, please," Fred said.

They received two white paper cones full of the strange-smelling nuts. Lindsay hadn't decided yet if the scent was pleasant or unpleasant, but it was potent. And the cone was delightfully warm. She cupped her hands around it.

Fred paid for the chestnuts. He'd paid for the carriage ride, too, while Lindsay had been digging in her purse for her wallet. It struck her as odd that not only did he have modern American currency, he had no trouble using it.

"Fred, how do you—"

"Try your monkeys' brains, before they get cold."

Lindsay tentatively peeled away a chestnut shell, so thin that it was more like a skin. Inside, it looked dark and shriveled, not much different from the ones that had come out of her oven. She took a bite and found the flavor more roasty than the ones she'd tried to cook at home, but she still couldn't tell whether she liked it or not.

Fred peered down at her. "Well? What do you think?"

She hadn't seen a man this concerned about the way she felt since Phil sent her home with strep throat last year. At least, not until she fainted in her own apartment a few nights ago.

"I'm not sure." She tried another one. They continued down the crowded sidewalk, and Lindsay ate one nut after the other while she tried to decide.

She never knew which direction to look. They

paused at some of the innumerable carts selling an array of handmade Christmas ornaments, candles, and other gifts. They caught the end of a children's puppet show of *The Night Before Christmas,* and a cluster of half a dozen men and women playing "Ding Dong Merrily on High" on handbells. Then, at a little kiosk near the end of the street, Lindsay bought the perfect Christmas present for her mother: a delicate deer figurine, made from blown glass.

That find, by itself, would have made the trip worthwhile. But it couldn't, by itself, account for the lightness Lindsay felt. She should be home addressing Christmas cards. Instead, despite the crowds and the cold, when they reached the end of the street where the little street fair broke off, she felt a sharp sense of disappointment. From here, a carriage would take them to the parking lot, where her familiar green Honda waited. She found herself reluctant to leave this little world behind. She wasn't sure how much of it was the street fair, and how much of it was the unlikely, charming man at her side.

"Here's what you need." A gentle squeeze at her elbow steered her toward the open doorway of a little coffee house. Lindsay felt the breath of its warmth before they actually stepped inside. The place was packed with people clustered around the tiny round tables. Yet, somehow, Fred found an empty table at the window, and a waitress arrived to take their order with equally surprising speed.

"Hot chocolate?" Fred lifted an eyebrow at her.

"Yes, please." Lindsay turned hopeful eyes toward the waitress. The lines around the woman's broad face and mouth didn't invite special orders, but Lindsay took a deep breath and tried anyway. "And could you please add a dash of vanilla? With whipped cream on top?"

At the woman's weary look, she immediately regretted the request. Until Fred added with a smile, "And the same for me, please."

The waitress returned his smile, and fifteen years fell away from her face. "No problem," she said, and headed back to the ordering counter with a light step.

Well, fine, Lindsay thought. *I said please, too.*

Still smiling, Fred eased back in the tiny, straight wooden chair, somehow managing to make it look comfortable. He folded his arms. "Vanilla." His eyes sparkled with amusement. "I still haven't figured you out."

Figured *me* out? "It's good that way. It makes the hot chocolate a little richer."

"Oh, I don't doubt it. That's why I ordered the same thing." He tipped his chair back slightly, a dangerous move in Lindsay's opinion, given its flimsy frame. "Your fudge recipe was delicious, too. The one piece I was able to eat, at any rate." His brows drew down ever so slightly, but not enough to quench the smile. "You definitely know how to add that little something extra, to make something more enjoyable."

It sounded like a compliment. Maybe that was what made Lindsay's cheeks heat, even as she waited for the other shoe to drop. Instead, he regarded her steadily until she was certain he could see inside of her. When she couldn't stand it any more, she prompted him: "But?"

His gaze shifted over her shoulder, and Lindsay turned to follow it.

A boy, probably about nine years old, carrying a handled cardboard box, edged his way down the row of tables alongside the window. Lindsay recognized the box and knew she'd soon be the owner of a couple of new candy bars. On any other night, the restaurant staff might have sent him off, but in the bustle of the Christmas festival, apparently no one had objected so far.

The boy reached their table and rested the box on the edge. "Would you like to buy a candy bar?" His hazel eyes and his question were aimed at Lindsay, probably figuring her for the soft touch she was. She pulled her purse into her lap.

But Fred answered first. "How many do you have left?"

He peered into his box. "Four."

"I'll take the rest." Fred reached into his pocket

and paid the boy, then accepted the candy bars. "Oh, here." He held one white-wrapped candy bar out to the boy. "You gave me one too many."

The boy counted the four candy bars still on the table. "There were only four."

"Well, then, this one must be for you." Fred winked.

The boy glanced from the candy bar in Fred's hand to the four on the table. "How'd you do that?"

"You've put in a good night's work. You deserve it."

"Thanks." He picked up his empty cardboard box and studied Fred. Finally, he said, "I have an uncle who can pull a quarter out of my ear."

"Really?" Fred looked astonished. "Why, that's the hardest trick of all."

As the little boy left with his empty box, he glanced back over his shoulder at Fred, his eyes notably rounder than they'd been when he came in.

Chapter 5

"So," Fred said, "you have urchins selling candy in the streets, in this day and age?"

"Not exactly." Lindsay followed Fred's gaze to the windowpane, where the boy stopped outside for a final, unabashed stare before he continued down the sidewalk away from the restaurant. "Here, they have to do it for school fund-raisers."

She grappled with a sudden disquiet. In the festive Christmas setting, everything had seemed so fitting, she'd almost forgotten the strange circumstances that had brought Fred into her life. But somewhere between the mysterious candy bars and the modern American currency and the mention of street urchins, her mind started swirling again. Who, or what, *was* he? With Fred's eyes off her, Lindsay caught herself staring at those smooth, impeccable features.

She shouldn't ask. Especially not in the middle of a crowded coffee house. But no one seemed to be paying any particular attention to them, and she doubted her words would carry far in the steady hum of chatter. "Fred, where did you come from, really?"

He turned back to her, eyebrows lifted. "Again? I thought we'd been through all that."

Lindsay wasn't going to be so easily put off. Questions darted through her head, any one of which was guaranteed to give her a headache. She grasped for the simplest one. "Where do you get money?"

He shrugged. "Is that all? I generally find I have what I need. Now, if I reached into my pocket because I thought I *needed* the down payment for a Rolls Royce, I have a feeling I'd be disappointed." He leaned back, allowing one arm to rest loosely on the back of his chair. "And here I thought I was going to have to explain something complicated, like the art of making candy bars appear. You worry about the strangest things, Lindsay."

Maybe because it was easier to think about something practical like money than how fund-raiser candy bars could materialize out of thin air.

His cajoling smile faded. "Do you get headaches very often?"

Lindsay lowered her hand from her temple, only now aware that she'd been rubbing it. "Not until you came along."

"It's all because you're much too serious." His

voice brushed over her ears like velvet. "Why not accept things as they are? You should know by now you're not getting rid of me. Not until December twenty-fifth, anyway."

That jarred her. "What—"

Fred nodded over her shoulder. "Here's just what the doctor ordered."

Lindsay looked up to see their waitress arrive with two tall glass pedestal mugs of hot chocolate, topped with whipped cream. She set the mugs down and smiled. At Fred. Whose dollop of whipped cream was distinctly bigger than the one on Lindsay's mug.

The waitress left. Wordlessly, Fred slid his mug across the table toward Lindsay, taking the one with less whipped cream for himself. He looked as if he were biting the inside of his lip again, this time in an effort to hold back a smile.

Lindsay held his solemn stare for as long as she could before she gave in and grinned, shaking her head. Her beginnings of a headache eased. She took her first sip of hot chocolate, then held the mug in front of her face while she quickly licked the whipped cream from her upper lip.

Fred managed his first drink with no problem, and somehow, without picking up a whipped cream moustache. "Perfect." He set down his mug. "How can anyone who knows enough to add vanilla to hot chocolate have trouble enjoying something as fine as Christmas?"

Lindsay sighed. "I guess it's all the deadlines." Fred propped his chin on his fist, as if he were listening to something fascinating. "I think part of it is just something that happens when you're an adult. When I was a kid, I remember counting down the days. Ten days till Christmas seemed like forever. Now, that's right about the time I start to panic. When you're a kid, you just enjoy Christmas. When you're a grown-up, it turns into this big to-do list. The cards, the presents, the fudge—"

"Well, you've heard my lecture on that."

"But a person can't just stop doing all those things. Everybody would think I was antisocial."

"And it wouldn't be any fun, either. If you decided not to participate at all, I guarantee, you'd be miserable. The key is to find a happy balance. Simpler ways to do things. You make everything so difficult." He shook his head. "Envelopes in your own handwriting. And I'll bet each of the notes has to be different too, just in case Aunt Betty calls Aunt Arline and reads her card over the phone."

Lindsay's mug froze on the way to her lips.

His eyes gleamed. "I knew it. Lindsay, do you think that child in Bethlehem cares how many cards you send out, or whether you have a tree up? Those things are meant to help you remember the holiday, not be swallowed up in it. It's supposed to be a time of joy, and you go about it with such grim purpose. 'I'm going to have a merry Christmas this time even if it kills me.'"

Lindsay took a deep drink of her hot chocolate. But she could only hide behind her mug for so long. When she lowered it, Fred was watching her, eyes contemplative. For the moment, any trace of teasing seemed to be gone.

"I just figured out what you are," he said.

"What?"

"You're a present." He nodded as if in satisfaction. "Tightly wrapped, with lots of tape, lots of beautiful shiny ribbon, all tied up in impossible knots. The kind of present that makes you half mad when you're trying to get it open. Because you know, the whole time, what's inside is going to be wonderful."

He studied her, so long and so steadily that she ducked her head as she scooped out a spoonful of whipped cream. "I told you before," she said. "You don't know me."

"I'm learning. Unwrapping the present."

When she raised her head, his eyes were still on her. There was something heavy in that stare. Something more than attentiveness, or interest. He looked—

He shook his head, and the look was gone. "Excuse me. Lost my train of thought. So tell me.

What was the nicest Christmas present you ever received?"

Lindsay flinched. "The nicest? Or the best?"

He gave her a puzzled look. "Your favorite."

"Well, the tape recorder was awfully nice, even if I did ruin the surprise. I used that thing for years, taping songs off the radio. And I learned something, too." She fingered the base of her mug. "You were right. I never peeked again."

"So that's not the year Christmas went south for you."

"Does it have to be any one year?"

"I suppose not."

Lindsay smelled a personal question coming up and tried to dodge it. "What about you? What's the nicest Christmas present you ever got?"

It worked. For possibly the first time, Fred seemed to be caught off guard. "Me? Not much point, my dear."

"What do you mean?"

"Think about it. Suppose someone gave me a sweater, and my next case calls for me to be a jockey. Or a football player. Or a trained seal. It would never fit."

She couldn't help grinning at that.

"There," he said. "*That's* something I can take with me."

"What?"

"Your smile." He was smiling himself as he said

it, but something in his eyes was serious. The longer they sat across the table from each other, the longer their stares seemed to get. Lindsay went for another scoop of whipped cream and found it had dissolved into a thin white foam at the top of her hot chocolate.

"Enough about me," he said. "Where does Steven figure in?"

Lindsay's throat tightened. "I don't want to talk about it."

"Come, now. This is going to look very bad on my performance review. Can you do me a favor?"

He touched her hand. Barely. He laid his fingertips lightly over her hand where it rested on the table, and Lindsay's pulse skittered. That single touch brought her eyes back to his and made it impossible to look away.

"Take one small step." His fingertips traced the back of her hand, still barely touching it. "Tell me one thing about Steven and I'll drop the subject for the rest of the night."

Lindsay licked her lips. He was touching her like that, and she was supposed to think about Steven?

"Let me guess." He gave her hand a gentle squeeze, eyes glimmering. "He's seven feet tall, with red eyes and arms the size of tree trunks."

"No." At least that helped her remember something about Steven. "His eyes were blue."

"Too easy. Doesn't count." Fred released her hand. "Lindsay, if you could see yourself. You look like a poker player trying with all her might to give up the worst card in the deck."

At least now that he'd let go of her hand, she could think. A little. "He was nice."

Fred drummed his fingers on the table, his eyes fixed on her face, a clear signal she wasn't going to get off that cheaply.

"Okay." Lindsay tried to think harder. Fred waited, not moving, clearly ready to listen—ready, she was sure, to be sympathetic. He'd automatically assumed she was the injured party, and no other thought appeared to have entered his mind. He only seemed to see good in her. And wasn't that what she wanted everyone to see?

If she ever told him what really happened, he wouldn't look at her that way anymore. It shouldn't matter. But somewhere, somehow, in the past few days, she'd started to care what he thought of her. When he shouldn't even exist, and she shouldn't even be sitting here with him.

She said, "We broke up a few days after Christmas."

It sounded like a lot. But it really didn't say anything.

And, as expected, Fred's face filled with compassion. "That explains a lot."

Hot chocolate turned to burning lava in her

stomach. Lindsay slid her hand off the table as Fred leaned forward.

"All right," he said softly. "I'm a man of my word. No more tonight. But we do have to talk about it sooner or later, you know."

Fine. He wanted to set her up with her ex-boyfriend. So why did he keep giving her looks that made her heart threaten to melt into her shoes? "What happens if I don't go along with all this?"

He shrugged, lifted his mug once again. "I'd be fired, I suppose." His eyes were guileless, a transparent ploy to play on her sympathy.

"Fired? What does that mean?"

"My dear, I have no idea. Banished to outer Mongolia, maybe. Or vanished into a puff of smoke. But it's not going to happen."

She frowned. "How do you know?"

"Lindsay, relax. I've never heard of it happening." He raised his mug to her. "You won't let me down."

Lindsay cringed inside, and she wondered how he could be so sure.

The sidewalk leading to Lindsay's apartment stretched out gray-white in front of them, thanks to the bright moon overhead and the remaining snowdrifts on either side of the pavement. Lindsay slowed her steps, not sure what to expect when

91

they reached the front porch. The scene reminded her too much of a blind date, the kind that generally ended with that awkward clinch on the front porch. Did the situation carry that kind of association for Fred? Probably not. After all, it wasn't likely you could call this unconventional, if lovely, evening a date. For Fred, this was purely professional. She thought so, anyway.

So what would Fred do when they got to the door?

What did she *want* him to do?

She didn't know.

Lindsay handled the moment the same way she'd handled similar ones in the past. She prattled. "I think it might snow again." The brisk stillness did, in fact, hint that more snow might be on the way. She breathed deeply, sampling the air as if she were Colorado's leading meteorologist, able to gauge the weather sheerly through sense of smell. "Probably not tonight, though."

"Care to make another bet?"

She glanced up at him. Mistake. She wasn't ready for the impact of his dark eyes and that smile, even in the half-light. But even as stupidly nervous as she was, she couldn't help smiling back. "Your bets are rigged."

"You're catching on," he acknowledged.

They had almost reached the door. Keys. That

was it. Lindsay lowered her head and busied herself digging through her purse, as if its vinyl compartments offered someplace to hide. "So, you say, snow tonight?"

"No." A thoughtful pause, or at least it sounded thoughtful, as Lindsay kept her eyes fixed on the key ring she'd just fished out from under her wallet. "Not for another few days. But I predict you'll have a white Christmas."

"That could make it hard to get to my parents' house."

"A white Christmas with clear roads, then."

Could he possibly arrange the weather? She'd wondered, briefly, if Fred could have had anything to do with the storm that had snowed her in yesterday. Another question she didn't really want to ask. Lindsay fumbled with her keys, concentrating with all her might on getting the right one into the doorknob. It was nearly as difficult as she tried to make it look; her fingers were half-numb, and the porch light was turned off.

"Oh, for goodness' sake, let me." If Fred was nervous, or had any idea of the thoughts circling through her head, his tone didn't show it. He reached for the doorknob, and Lindsay moved her hand as though dodging fire.

He opened the door and, to Lindsay's surprise, swept past her into the apartment. At first it seemed like an unprecedented breach of his usual gentlemanly etiquette. But no. Fred appeared to be exercising an even more ancient manly ritual, checking the household for intruders.

He flicked on the entryway light—the one where he'd hung the mistletoe—and motioned her inside. Then he strode away, skirting past the mistletoe, and started turning on the rest of the lights. First, in the living room, beginning with the lights on her Christmas tree. Then the kitchen. And then, down the hall, to the bedroom.

Lindsay walked past the dangerous mistletoe and waited beside the couch for Fred's return. No way was she following him into the bedroom.

Did he really feel the need to check the apartment, or could he possibly be as uncertain as she was?

He returned from the bedroom with a smile, turning off lights behind him as he went. "All clear. Not even any monsters under the bed. I checked." As if she'd asked him to.

He'd handily avoided the front porch ritual. But now he still had to find his way out of her apartment. Lindsay would have found it amusing, if her heart hadn't been thrumming in her throat. And at this point, she was starting to feel a little insulted. *Come on, Fred,* a ticklish little demon in her brain sneered. *It's not like I have the Black Plague or something.*

He stood at the edge of her living room, two steps away from Lindsay and several long strides away from the front door. Fred contemplated her, then the door. He'd have to pass the mistletoe again to get to it. His eyes returned to Lindsay. And stayed there.

He knew, all right. The weight of that stare threatened to hold her pinned to the spot for all eternity, or at least until she crumpled to the floor. Lindsay felt drawn in by that dark-eyed gaze, tempted to take a step forward and close part of the space between them. But it would have to be his move, because right now her legs didn't seem able to do anything she told them.

"Did you have a nice time tonight?" His voice was no quieter than usual, yet it had the feel of an intimate whisper.

"Yes." She must have been desperate to fill the building silence, because she heard herself jabber, "I wish this wasn't all business." *Idiot.*

"All business? For me, there's no such thing." He stepped forward. Less than arm's length away now. "This isn't random. I was chosen for your case for some very special reason." Reaching up, he ran the outside of one finger lightly, excruciatingly, along her cheek. "Believe me, there's no other place I would have rather been tonight."

She believed him implicitly. Those heavy dark eyes held no trace of artifice.

His touch lingered on her cheek. Just one finger, and it threatened to be her undoing. Lindsay half-closed her eyes, ready for whatever came next.

Or so she thought.

"I haven't given you my lesson in proper Christmas tree appreciation, have I?" he said.

His tone was much more conversational, bringing Lindsay's eyes wide open again. "I don't think so."

"Let me put it this way. Have you spent any time looking at your tree since we put it up?"

"I've barely been home."

"Then you're missing out. And you're not letting your tree do its job. I'll show you what I mean." Any sign of hesitancy gone, he took her by the shoulders and steered her to the couch, pressing down gently but firmly until she sat. She was too confused to resist. Fred crossed the room to douse the main light switch. Now the only illumination came from the lights on the tree, and a faint glow from the kitchen beyond. Fred perched on the arm of the couch, next to her but slightly behind her, just out of her line of sight. His hands rested on her shoulders again. "I almost forgot. Music."

Lindsay felt a movement behind her, as though he'd nodded, and her stereo clicked on. Her shoulders jumped under his hands. "Sorry," he said, squeezing her shoulders lightly. "It's the only way I'll ever master that stereo of yours."

The CD she'd left in the player yesterday started up, an acoustic guitar playing "The First Noel."

"Nice choice," he murmured. He rubbed her shoulders lightly, as though he could feel the tension there. "Relax. There's nothing so strange about a little magic at Christmas. Don't forget, all of Christmas is built on the most magical thing that ever took place."

"What are you . . ."

"Hush. Remember, eyes on the tree."

She'd been staring at the blue readout lights on the front of her stereo. Lindsay pulled her gaze away and focused on the tree.

"Now," he said. His voice was soothing, and so was the warmth of his breath at the top of her head. "Here's the hard part for you. Don't think. That is, don't think about work, or mailing cards, or shopping. Think of that first Christmas. Of all the best Christmases you've known. Little moments, big ones . . . this year, last year . . . It's all part of one large, beautiful thing. Just let it wash over you. Feel it. Enjoy it."

His hands stilled on her shoulders. The room went still, too, except for the carols playing quietly in the background. There seemed to be nothing else to do but drink in the sight of the Christmas tree. Its bright bulbs, the chief source of light in the room, illuminated her ornaments, new and old, in a haphazard jumble. Rudolph, the ballerinas, and the old silver star at the top. The green scent of pine, the gentle weight of Fred's touch on her shoulders, the soothing Christmas melody. It was all part of this moment, and as she gazed across the room, Lindsay allowed her eyes to go slightly out of focus so that the tree was a soft blur of color.

"There." The gentle baritone voice caressed her ears, and Lindsay felt a rare contentment. She wasn't sure where it came from, the man behind her or the tree in front of her, but it felt as if she could sit here, hour after hour, and still not a minute of time would pass.

She was, she realized, completely in the present.

She had no idea how long they sat that way before Fred moved, slowly, as if afraid to disturb her. When she started to turn, his hands on her shoulders stilled her once again.

"Don't move," he whispered. He leaned forward, and Lindsay felt the brush of a kiss at her temple. "Good night, darling." His kiss, and his voice at her ear, sent a warm shiver through her. She never would have thought a shiver could be warm, but this one was.

He rose, and the space where he'd been felt cold and vacant behind her. Lindsay tried to move, but her limbs seemed to have turned to syrup and wouldn't obey her.

Before she could even begin to get up, she heard the front door close after him.

He hadn't expected to be summoned to Headquarters so abruptly.

Usually he reported in of his own volition. Which, come to think of it, he hadn't done in the past couple of days. Not since they'd given him his instructions about Lindsay and Steven.

One moment he was strolling down the street away from Lindsay's apartment. The next, he was—not.

How are things going on the Lindsay Miller case? His supervisor wasted no time.

Fine. He composed his thoughts, still trying to adjust. This wasn't the way they normally did things; being jerked out of the physical realm without warning had left him disoriented. He tried to compose himself. *I think we made some good progress tonight.*

I hope so. Time is short. What sort of progress?

He found, once again, he didn't want to share details. Since when did Headquarters micromanage, anyway? *I think she's beginning to see the value in focusing on the present.* There. He couldn't help but convey his satisfaction in that.

What about the past?

He hesitated, wishing he could take a deep

breath. Strange, having the urge to breathe when you didn't have a body at the moment.

His supervisor reminded him: *Before she can truly live in the present, she needs to correct her past mistakes.*

The past sends her running the other way. It wouldn't be wise to press—

Perhaps you still need to earn her trust. Perhaps she's suspicious of your motives.

This time he really felt the need to struggle for air. He started to say, *My motives are as pure as the day is long—*

And then he was gasping for breath, drawing in gulps of the cold air that suddenly surrounded him. It surprised him what a relief it was to be solid again, even if it left him doubled over and panting.

He was back at Lindsay's front door. The porch light was out, and at first he thought she'd retired for the night. But no. The lighted Christmas tree glowed through her living room window, with another light beyond it.

Fred stepped back, his footstep betraying him on the crunching snow. Footstep? He didn't need feet, not out here. He didn't need his body at all. He'd been abruptly thrown back into it, as suddenly as it had been taken away from him.

It had *never* happened this way before.

He stepped back again, more quietly this time. A simple matter to be gone again, or remain here unseen—just wish it so—but he found he wanted to catch a better glimpse with his eyes, through that lighted window.

Then the front door cracked open, the sound of the wood in the jamb magnified to a rifle shot. She'd heard something, probably his asthmatic wheezing when he first reappeared on her porch. He winked out of his physical form again before the door opened.

It didn't open far. About six inches, and he could see her face inside, trying to peer out without stepping forward. Was she that afraid of him? Or the threat of some unknown intruder?

She opened the door a little farther to poke her head out. Belatedly, the porch light flicked on, bathing her head in a light golden glow.

"Hello?" Lindsay's eyes searched the darkness beyond the porch light, her eyes falling directly on the spot where he would have stood, if he'd been standing. Coincidence? Her eyes remained fixed there for a moment, and she stepped forward, hugging her arms around her bright red sweater. It felt like the most natural thing in the world to reach out for her, to soothe away the cold and apprehension. Except, of course, that appearing in front of her would send her screaming inside and destroy all his work so far.

She looked so alone. In the apartment beyond her, he saw a few stray cards scattered on the floor, as if they'd tumbled from the tray when she got up. He had a good idea what she'd been up to since he left.

Lindsay's eyes lingered on his vantage point for several more seconds. Then she ducked back in and closed the door, which had never been open more than a foot.

She could have sworn she'd heard someone outside.

Lindsay bolted the door and started back toward the tray of cards, but she couldn't bring herself to sit down again. Maybe she'd been imagining noises just to avoid the task. She certainly hadn't been making much headway.

Fred might be bringing out her Christmas spirit, but he wasn't helping her concentration. She detoured to the refrigerator and the carton of eggnog. It had expired yesterday. Lindsay sniffed the contents, decided to take a chance, and poured a mug. She added nutmeg and took a cautious sip. Still good.

She returned to the living room and sat close to the fire, realizing that Fred would approve. He was getting under her skin, like some kind of posthypnotic suggestion. But surely, taking a little good advice couldn't be wrong.

Lindsay turned her gaze to the tree again. That part was harder to recapture. She'd turned too many lights on. And this time she didn't have warm hands on her shoulders, a soothing voice, or a soft kiss beside her ear.

She sipped the eggnog again, slowly, and tried to quiet the buzzing thoughts inside her head.

Cards. Shopping. *Christmas tree. Glowing lights. Fred* . . .

Steven.

He was waiting there, at the back of her mind, like a bill to be paid. If Fred was really here to get her to fix things with Steven, it was a high price to pay. And she couldn't imagine how she'd go about it.

Had she really made a mistake ten years ago? She knew she'd handled the end of their relationship badly, and she had to admit, it would be nice to know how Steven was doing now. But for all the times she'd wondered about him, she'd never really thought about going back to him. She just wished she hadn't hurt him.

In the years since then, dating had been a process of dipping her toe into the water only to jerk it back. She didn't want to go in too deep, didn't want to start something she couldn't finish.

Lindsay sighed, sipped her eggnog again, and realized she wasn't even seeing the tree, although her eyes were aimed right at it. She needed something more distracting. She reached for the remote control and turned on the television set.

A *Christmas Carol* was showing again. No surprise there. Two different versions, in fact. She'd never be able to see that movie the same way again, no matter what Fred looked like. Lindsay scrolled through the menu, searching for something less close to home. *It's a Wonderful Life?* Too many regrets. *Miracle on 34th Street,* featuring a cynical career woman who didn't believe in love or Santa Claus . . . no, not tonight.

Finally she found an old Bing Crosby special. That would do it. Lindsay turned up the volume, tucked her feet up under her, and did her best to ignore the Christmas cards.

Chapter 6

The next morning, Lindsay got to her desk promptly at nine. At five minutes after nine, a hand dropped from out of nowhere onto her stack of papers. A large, square-cut diamond ring flared at her.

She looked up from the hand into Jeanne's face, which was also sparkling.

"What—!" Lindsay stood and sent her chair rolling backward. Her eyes went from the flashing ring to Jeanne's face one more time. "Brad?"

Jeanne nodded, still beaming. "Guess he decided not to cheap out for Christmas after all."

"Congratulations!" Lindsay crunched her friend into a hug, still trying to take it all in. She'd only met Brad once or twice, and he wouldn't have been her first choice, what with his penchant for televised sports, cheap burgers, and sudden arguments. But if Jeanne was happy, so was she.

Lindsay wondered, fleetingly, if the big, chunky

stone was cubic zirconia, then stomped the thought down. *As long as Jeanne's happy,* she reminded herself.

She pulled back, allowing her friend to breathe. "Tell me how it happened! Were you expecting anything like this?"

Jeanne shook her head, still smiling from ear to ear. "Not in a million years."

And Lindsay saw it. Or she thought she did. A shady flicker, just beneath the brightness in Jeanne's eyes. Lindsay felt a chill of recognition as Jeanne continued.

"We were on our way out to dinner," she said. "He just fished into his pocket and brought out this black velvet box. . . ."

The details faded from Lindsay's hearing. Because when someone surprised you with a box containing a diamond ring, she knew from experience, there was only one answer that came easily.

"—and what else could I say?" Jeanne finished, with the same big smile firmly in place. The longer Lindsay saw it, the more she sensed the underlying effort behind it. That flicker of doubt.

She could be imagining it.

"I've never been so surprised in my life," Jeanne added.

No. It wasn't her imagination.

Lindsay kept her own smile in place as well. She didn't know what else to do.

It hounded her through the morning. Not just

the vision of Jeanne bringing drinks and chips to a couch potato who wouldn't even say "Thank you"—because, after all, Lindsay didn't know that was the way Jeanne's marriage would turn out. She just strongly suspected it.

What really bothered her was the nagging suspicion that Jeanne knew, deep down, that she was making a mistake. A mistake Jeanne didn't want to admit to anyone, least of all herself. The same mistake Lindsay had nearly made with Steven ten years ago, before she returned his ring and ran out on him.

She'd solved her problem, all right. In a way that guaranteed Steven would never want to see her again. A shabby end to a pleasant four-year relationship.

Pleasant. Now, there was a bland word. Had that been the problem all along?

Lindsay tried to think back on her time with Steven as she slogged through her morning's work. Four years together, and she couldn't remember a single argument. He'd been considerate and dependable. They'd griped about the same teachers, seen the same movies together, and, more often than not, they'd helped decorate each other's Christmas trees. *Pleasant.* What was so wrong with that?

Lindsay thought of the little current that had passed between her and Fred, just from the brush of his finger on her cheek. Then the relaxed contentment of gazing at the tree with his hands resting on her shoulders. Making fudge, walking together on a snow-flanked sidewalk . . . surely all of that was *pleasant,* too. But it was something more.

Now she was comparing Steven with an Englishman who'd appeared in her life out of thin air. As if anything real could come out of that.

Even if she was right about Jeanne, who was Lindsay to give advice?

Lindsay sighed and looked at her watch. Nearly lunchtime. She wouldn't be going out for Thai food today; that was a rare splurge, and Jeanne was meeting Brad for lunch to celebrate. Lindsay pulled open her drawer and eyed the sandwich she'd brought yesterday, but day-old peanut butter looked far less inviting than a chance to get out of the office for a while. Maybe a change of scenery would help her get away from thoughts of ex-boyfriends, glittering diamond rings, and that hint of dimness in Jeanne's smile.

Lindsay went to the food court at the mall nearby. She could grab some fast food, and maybe she'd manage some quick Christmas shopping after she gobbled her chicken nuggets.

Predictably, this close to Christmas, the food court was thick with people. As Lindsay stood in line, she went through her gift list mentally: Jeanne, Phil, Evelyn, Matt . . . what could she come up with

108

that she hadn't already given them before? It got harder every year to find new inspiration. And every year, it seemed like she got a little closer to the wire. Maybe this was the year she should just buy gift cards and get it over with.

The mall's Muzak reached her ears, singing about growing a little leaner, a little older, a little sadder . . . a little colder.

Great. Now even Johnny Mathis was picking on her.

Lindsay got through the line, turned to search for a seat, and her food tray nearly collided with a familiar charcoal-black overcoat.

Fred steadied the tray as Lindsay staggered off balance.

One glance told him this wasn't the same woman he'd left sitting contentedly on her couch last night. Her eyes—that clear, light gray that usually reminded him of snowflakes—were more like storm clouds today, troubled and shadowy. Fred felt his own mood dim slightly, and that was a foreign sensation to him. But he didn't like seeing her so disquieted.

Lindsay barely looked up at him. "Not now, Fred," she said, and started to pull the tray away.

Not good. Not good at all. She didn't even seem surprised to see him. Either she was getting very blasé about this whole thing, or something was truly distressing her. He tried not to dwell on how much her mood unsettled him, or what his own reaction might mean.

He held firmly to the tray. "Not so fast. What's wrong?"

She tugged at the tray again. "Fred, seriously. I'm not in the mood."

"I can see that. What happened?"

"I don't want to talk about it."

This could be a splendid opportunity, as good a glance into Lindsay's inner demons as he was ever likely to get, but that wasn't what kept his grip so tenaciously on her tray. He didn't like that cloudy look in her eyes, as if she really weren't seeing him at all. That troubled crease between her eyebrows. Laugh lines were fine, but that crease didn't belong there. He yearned to rub it away, as if he could erase it with his thumb.

He held on to her gaze as firmly as he could. "Let's sit down."

Her eyes regained a little of their focus, and she relinquished the tray. Good. He'd reached her, at least a little.

Finding a seat in this mass of humanity could be a trick. The food court resembled a parking lot of tables, with little more space between them than so many parked cars. But that was a problem much more easily solved than Lindsay's troubled mood.

A few feet away, Fred glimpsed two young

women lingering needlessly over two nearly-empty drink cups, and kept his eyes there; a moment later they both stood, still chatting, never consciously aware of his gaze. Fred held one of the newly vacated chairs out for Lindsay, then took his seat across from her.

She preoccupied herself arranging the items on the brown plastic tray in front of her. Then her eyes flicked up. "How'd you find me here?"

Unimportant details again. "Maybe because you needed me. I'm here for you, remember?"

Light brown eyelashes lowered. A sure sign she had something to say, and didn't want to say it.

He fought off the temptation to reach for her hand. "So, what's this thing you don't want to talk about?"

She bit into one of the strange-looking breaded chunks from her tray a little more fiercely than seemed necessary. "I just found out Jeanne's getting married."

"And?"

She stared at the remaining bit of breaded food in her hand, as if she too wondered what it was. "I think maybe she's making a mistake."

"How so?"

Lindsay shrugged. "I just don't think he's right for her, that's all."

"How would you know that?"

She met his eyes for the first time since they'd

sat down. "Fred, this is the guy she was afraid was going to break up with her just to save money on a Christmas present. He wasn't even with her at the company party. Probably home watching a football game." The rest of the morsel met the same violent fate as its predecessor.

"I don't understand. You're upset because your friend is throwing her life away on a monster who watches sports programs? Sounds like the fate of half the women in America to me."

Her eyebrows arched. "Are British men any better?"

"You're forgetting. I'm not really British, or American, or anything else. And you're changing the subject." Rather smoothly, he had to admit. "Although I don't have much use for television. Now, if I could figure out how to make the thing work, why then, there might be trouble."

She cracked a smile. Better. "It's nice to make you smile," he said, before he thought.

Confusion crept into her face, and he remembered his abrupt visit to Headquarters last night. He had to be more careful what he said. And not let her distract him from the matter at hand, whether with that smile, or her little changes of subject.

"Lindsay, what's really bothering you about this? Could it have anything to do with the fact that Jeanne is getting married and you're not?"

Her eyes flashed. "You're way off."

"Methinks thou dost protest too much."

The stormy look in her eyes turned to utter frost. Fred rather admired the spirit behind that glare. Anything was better than the vacant, preoccupied look she'd worn when he first ran into her. He searched her chilly gaze without backing down, trying to ascertain what lay behind it. Begrudge a friend her happiness? No, it didn't sound like the Lindsay he knew. But then, emotions weren't always rational, and if Lindsay did feel jealous, she might also feel guilty about it. That could account for her mood, and her defensiveness about it. Fred studied her, weighing her expression as best he could.

No. It was the obvious reaction, but it didn't feel right. He said softly, still holding her gaze, "What is it then?"

The troubled crease between her brows deepened. She ducked her head to take a drink from her cup. As her lips pursed around the straw, Fred couldn't help imagining how a good kiss would help them both forget all this nonsense. He shouldn't be thinking this way, and he knew it. He couldn't remember ever—

"She's my friend." Lindsay's eyes drifted past his shoulder, almost as if she were speaking to someone else. "I think she's doing the wrong thing. But it's not for me to say." She toyed with her straw. "I don't think she's really in love with him."

113

Fred stayed motionless, almost afraid to speak out loud. "What makes you say that?"

Lindsay shook her head, light brown waves of hair swaying slightly around her face. "Just a feeling."

"Then why would she say yes? There's not that much social pressure on a woman to get married these days, is there?"

"More than you think. There's the whole biological clock thing. And there's just something about a diamond ring—" Her eyes remained fixed over his shoulder. "Just the fact that someone would give it to you."

She sat up straighter, drawing farther back from him. Her tone changed. "Maybe you're right. Maybe I am a little jealous." She searched out another breaded chunk of food from her tray.

"You know, I don't believe you've ever lied to me before."

Her eyes came up to meet his. Her lips parted, as if to deny it, but nothing came out.

He was close to something here. So close, he could practically step on it. But if he stepped too hard, he might crush it.

"All right," Fred said. "Here's a harder question."

She looked at him warily over her cup.

He said, "What are those things in front of you?"

She plucked up one of the breaded bits. "They're chicken nuggets. I guess they take chicken and—"

He frowned. "Grind it up? And cover it with bread? I thought this was a civilized society."

It had the desired effect. It made her laugh, and for the moment that troublesome line between her brows disappeared. "I don't understand you, Fred. You know who Bing Crosby is, but you don't know what chicken nuggets are?"

"Need-to-know basis, remember."

"So, what, is there a manual or something?"

"Not really. It's sort of like the way . . . Can you remember the first time you heard 'Silent Night'? You know it because you've always known it. I know who Bing Crosby is the same way I know"—he cast around in his mind for an example, shrugged—"that *Gone with the Wind* is a film about the Civil War, where someone says a four-letter word at the end."

Lindsay buried her face in her hands. Had he said something wrong?

Then she brought her hands partway down and peered at him over her fingers. Her eyes brimmed, not with tears, but with mirth, and he loved the fact that he'd put it there. He didn't care one whit whether the joke was on him. "Oh, Fred. You're serious, aren't you?"

He shrugged. "Enlighten me."

She lowered her hands, shaking her head. "I can't. It's a three-hour movie."

"Maybe we could watch it together." He bit his tongue. As he'd been so recently reminded, time was short. A three-hour movie with Lindsay just wasn't in the offing. And she had him sidetracked again. Still, it seemed to him that this light, meaningless conversation did her more good than poking away at things she obviously found painful.

Apparently not. He had his orders. Even as he sat considering them, he saw the laughter fading from those light gray eyes, back toward her customary serious expression. How could Lindsay's best interest run so contrary to his own instincts?

Somewhere along the line, she'd demolished all but one of the chicken bits. Lindsay edged her chair backward. "I've got to go. If I hurry I might be able to get some Christmas shopping done before I have to get back to work."

"There you go again. If you *hurry*. Your thinking is all wrong. Besides which, you're going to chase your way to an early coronary before you reach thirty."

"I've got too much to do." The crease between her brows reappeared.

"Come shopping with me tonight. I promise you'll get twice as much done."

"I really need some time alone."

At least that was honest. "Understood. Just one thing, before you go."

Lindsay looked at him quizzically, halfway out of her seat. He held her eyes with his until she settled back into her chair.

Fred leaned across the table, resting his fingers lightly against her temple. "Close your eyes."

She hesitated, then did as he asked. Fred extended his thumb to rub at the fine little crease between her brows, willing away that tension, trying to get at the source of it. He could feel it, but he couldn't see it. After a moment it eased, and Lindsay's shoulders visibly relaxed. He lowered his hand. "That's better. You've had this little frown between your brows all afternoon and it's been driving me out of my mind."

She opened her eyes. She looked more relaxed, more like the woman he'd left on her couch last night. "What did you do?"

"Nothing major. Just getting rid of some of the tension. You could pay someone a lot of money to rub your neck and shoulders for the same result." He frowned, trying not to take it personally. "You still don't trust me, do you?"

She didn't answer. Her eyes were twin gray mirrors of confusion.

Fred reached up again and gave in to something he'd wanted to do for some time. He sank his fingers into that light brown hair of hers, gently smoothing it back from her temple. It was softer and lighter than he'd imagined, softer and lighter than the scarf he'd given her. He searched for more tension to soothe away, but this time he found himself caught in his own web. A sense of

117

warmth, of peace, descended on him, made him want to stay there indefinitely. It had its effect on Lindsay, too. She closed her eyes again, like a cat being stroked.

"Don't worry." He let his voice caress her along with his fingers. "I can't hypnotize you and I can't read your mind, more's the pity. My work would be a lot easier if I could."

At the mention of work, her eyes opened again. Drat. Why had he put it that way? Probably for the best, he decided. Better for all concerned if Lindsay thought his feelings for her were purely professional.

He broke the contact and did his best to make his tone more matter-of-fact. "So, I'll leave you alone for the afternoon. But you and I have an appointment to go shopping this evening. Understood?"

She nodded, like someone slowly awakening, and stood with her tray. "It's a deal," she said, and moved away. Fred tried to keep his eyes from following her as she dumped the contents of her tray into a waste bin and walked away. That preoccupied look stole over her face again—whether because of her friend Jeanne, or the overwhelming task of buying Christmas gifts, he didn't know.

He'd help her tonight. He grinned at an image of himself struggling under a stack of hatboxes. Or was that only in the movies? His cultural references were muddled, formed out of vague impressions that weren't even memories. No wonder the poor girl was confused.

Fred sat back in his chair, lingering in the food court to sample the bustling atmosphere of the mall around him. Some of it was happy. Much of it was frantic. The low rumble of voices nearly buried the Christmas music playing over the sound system.

He thought of Lindsay and her talk about deadlines. How had mankind managed to turn the birth of a savior into this?

Only one way to find out. Jump into the thick of it. And he knew the perfect way to do it. While she was still at work, he'd go shopping himself, and find Lindsay a Christmas present. But not with the help of any special skills. He'd do it her way—the hard way—and take a walk in her shoes.

After two hours, he began to understand what Lindsay was up against.

Producing the perfect striped scarf at a moment's notice was child's play compared to finding the right gift at a shopping mall. A hundred stores under one roof, and everything seemed either too personal, or not personal enough. And all of them, somehow, far too ordinary for Lindsay. Though money wasn't a consideration—if he found the right thing, he would find himself with the right amount of money—he didn't want to choose something too cheap, or too expensive.

The value of a gift implied an underlying meaning, despite the fact that it shouldn't.

So. Fred dropped his shoulders, momentarily at a loss. He'd take this exercise one step further, and ask for help. Not from a salesperson, though. His eyes fell on a woman with a stroller, who'd paused to rest on a bench in front of one of the mall's little fountains. She looked about Lindsay's age, and with a baby in tow, she wasn't likely to misunderstand his motives for approaching her.

As Fred walked up, the baby kicked and squealed under powder-blue blankets, and her mother rolled the stroller back and forth, trying to shush her.

"Are you giving your mother a rough time of it, young lady?"

Both heads turned toward his voice. From the light in the mother's eyes, it appeared he'd already scored a point.

The woman smiled. "Usually people think she's a boy, especially when I take her out in the blue blanket."

"Unthinkable." Fred regarded the little face in the stroller. About six months old, at a guess, with sparkling eyes and a barely visible tuft of blond hair. Enchanting. "I'll bet she already has her father wrapped around her little finger."

A faint shadow crossed the woman's face, but it didn't dim her curiosity. "Where are you from?"

"Camden. It's an older part of London. But I

think I'm as lost in this mall as I've been anywhere since I got here."

She laughed, and her brown eyes lightened. "I've lived here two years, and I still get that way."

"I was hoping you might be able to shed some light for me. I'm trying to find a Christmas gift for a young woman. I haven't known her very long, but I'd still like to make it special, and I wasn't sure what would be appropriate."

She frowned, apparently more than willing to tackle a shopping question. "So, probably not jewelry."

"Probably not."

The baby jabbered excitedly. Fred frowned at her with mock sternness. "You're interrupting, young lady."

She kicked her legs with glee. And was quiet.

The woman tweaked the baby's chin, and a teasing gleam rose in her eyes. "Is this something you'd like to turn into . . . more?"

"Not in the cards, I'm afraid." To his surprise, the words came out with some difficulty. "I'll be . . . out of the country again in a few days. But I'd still like it to be something she'll remember."

The realization blindsided him with the force of a freight train. He'd just told her more than he knew himself.

"Hm," she said. "That's a toughie."

Fred's heart twisted. He tried to shake it off, the

best way he knew how. "How about you? What do you want most for Christmas?"

Some color came into her face. "A date with my husband."

"Really? And I would have guessed he was the one who thought you were too caught up in the baby."

Her color deepened. "I've been afraid to leave her with someone else so soon."

"Oh, she's ready. See that gleam in her eye? It says, 'I've got two helpless adults at my beck and call.' Do you have family in town?"

"My sister," she admitted.

"It's definitely time. Invite your husband out. I promise you he'll be thrilled."

Well, that handled things for one of them.

A few minutes later, with no new inspiration, Fred wished the woman a merry Christmas, and continued on his fool's errand.

He had a problem a lot bigger than finding the right gift. The only reason why he, the holiday expert, should be at such a sudden loss. Because it was so important. In a few days he'd be gone, and he wanted something for Lindsay to remember him by.

Chapter 7

"You're hoarding the tape again."

Lindsay looked down to her left, and sure enough, the roll of adhesive tape was on the carpet beside her, right where Fred couldn't reach it. Unable to think of a snappy retort, she settled for a mock glare and tossed it back over to him where he sat, suitably enough, at the foot of her Christmas tree. Fred snatched it from the air with his free hand, then secured the green-and-gold flap on the present he was wrapping.

The shopping had gone better than she'd ever expected, despite the insane crowds at the mall. Crowds seemed to have a way of thinning for Fred, lines got shorter, and the harried clerks at the register tended to brighten after one look at him. Lindsay couldn't say she blamed them. He'd been making her laugh all evening. She could almost chalk the successful shopping up to Fred's natural charm, and a bit of good luck. If she didn't think about it too hard.

She found she didn't want to think about it too hard. It felt too natural to have Fred helping her in the perennial ritual of scissors, tape and ribbon, and he made it much more fun. Even her qualms about Jeanne's engagement had faded, for now at least. Maybe she'd just been projecting her own experience with Steven, after all.

The TV tray full of cards still stood in front of her sofa, looking down at them like a disapproving sentry. Tonight, Lindsay refused to worry about it. She was so late with them now, one more night of neglect barely seemed to matter. She probably wouldn't feel that way tomorrow. But she felt that way tonight, under the influence of the Christmas carols on her stereo, a successful evening's shopping, and the bright red and green wrapping paper strewn around her living room floor. Not to mention the presence of a relentlessly jolly man named Fred.

He hadn't even mentioned Steven. Lindsay entertained a flicker of hope, probably a naive one, that he might have given up on the subject.

"Who else is left on your shopping list?"

"Well, Jeanne. I suppose I should make it some kind of engagement present." Lindsay concentrated on the box she was now wrapping for Phil, a kitschy clock in the shape of a ship's wheel. "And then there's Matt—"

Fred snorted. "He's not getting what *he* wants."

Lindsay felt herself blush. She'd nearly forgotten Fred's comment the night of the Christmas party. "You were wrong about him, you know. The one he's got a crush on is Jeanne."

"I never said he didn't. Men are notorious window shoppers. I still say that given the least bit of encouragement, he'd—" He lowered his head and busied himself fixing the already-perfect gold bow on his package. "Never mind. You can't fault a man for having good taste."

Lindsay's heart responded with an unexpected *thump* of excitement. She held her breath.

Fred held up the box for her inspection. "There. How's that?"

She felt her face go a deeper red. "Beautiful." He'd made a light, flirty comment, that was all. It had meant nothing. But as Fred set the present under the tree with the others, her heartbeat had trouble slowing. She felt an urge to pay him back. "So what should I get Matt?"

"My dear, I don't have the faintest idea." His head remained turned away, apparently intent on finding just the right spot for this gift.

"You're the one who spotted the clock for Phil. And that sweater for my dad. He's always so hard to buy for." Fred still didn't answer. She needled, "You must have *some* ideas for Matt."

"Oh, I do." He turned back to her, the customary smile well in place. "But being a gentleman, I can't say them." He clasped his hands around his knee. "Have we wrapped everything?"

"Just about." Defeated, Lindsay turned her attention to the bow for Phil's present. With someone else to help, she'd gotten more elaborate with some of the packages tonight, adding on more ribbons and curlicues than she usually did. For this one, she slapped on a blue adhesive bow and slid the box across the floor to Fred. "Done."

Once again, he spent a long careful moment finding the right spot under the tree. Maybe he'd realized, as she had, that with the wrapping done, there was no other real pretext for him to stay.

"I suppose," Fred said, turning back to her, "with Jeanne getting married, Matt *really* isn't getting what he wanted for Christmas."

The teasing note had left his eyes, and his voice. "I suppose," Lindsay agreed.

He'd stopped avoiding her eyes, too. "How is it that you've never gotten married?"

Lindsay's heart did it again. *Thump.* She'd never known it to sound so huge, or so loud. "I'm only twenty-nine."

"Come on." A teasing flicker returned to his

eyes, a very gentle one. "Ten years on the market, and no one's been smart enough to snap you up?"

Thump thump. Thump. Lindsay tried to keep her voice normal, but it was hard to hear it over the noise of her heart. "I don't go out much. I haven't really been looking."

"Ah, but love is hardly ever found by *looking.*"

"What are you saying?"

"Just stating a fact. And I just hope you've never doubted that you have something special to offer."

Lindsay's racing heart gave a huge *thud,* as if for the last time.

Oh, great.

Fred wasn't flirting. He was giving her more amateur pop psychology. A boost to little Lindsay's self-esteem, his good deed for the night. When what she really wanted—

She launched herself to her feet and started wadding up stray scraps of wrapping paper with a vengeance. Then she made a beeline for the trash basket in the kitchen without looking at Fred.

She wanted him to kiss her. *That* was what she wanted. How humiliating.

When she finished stuffing the gift wrap as far down into the kitchen trash as it would go, and turned back around, of course he was standing right there. "Lindsay—"

He stopped. At least he knew better than to ask what was wrong. But he didn't know better than to keep his hands off her. He laid his hands on her shoulders, and something about the warmth in his touch kept her from shaking him off.

"Lindsay," he said again, and there was no way to avoid those dark eyes, so dangerously, annoyingly filled with understanding. "Listen. I'm supposed to know the right thing to say, and the fact that I'm botching it up so badly has to mean—"

That allowed her to jerk free. Clearly, he was still on the clock, and she didn't want to hear any more about his job description. She didn't care what kind of heavenly realm he came from; she didn't want to be a project anymore.

Lindsay strode to the door and picked up his overcoat from the back of the couch, where he'd tossed it when they came in. She wheeled around to hand him his coat; once again, as expected, Fred was standing right behind her. But this time he wasn't looking at her. He was looking up.

At the mistletoe, directly over their heads.

He met her eyes with a look that glimmered with promise. Then he took the overcoat from her hand and tossed it, lightly, onto the back of the sofa once again.

Everything seemed to slow. His intentions were clear, and she had plenty of time to step back. Yet Lindsay did nothing to stop him when he took her chin in his hand, tipped it upward, and brought his lips down to hers, as purposefully as if he'd meant to do it all along.

Lindsay could have sworn she heard bells.

She closed her eyes. She couldn't help it. At first the kiss was feather-light, but his lips closed more firmly over hers, drawing her closer, drawing her in. Her heartbeat, the one that had threatened to stop a few minutes ago, was making up for lost time. Fred's fingers wandered from her chin, reaching around the back of her head, slowly entangling themselves in her hair. His other arm slid around her waist, and Lindsay had never felt so completely *held* before.

When Fred lifted his head, he half-expected her to skitter away, but she stayed in front of him, her face still upturned, soft brown eyelashes lowered. It would have been impossible for him to pull back. So he brought his lips down to hers again for a deeper kiss, and a sensation that was so indescribably sweet it nearly took his knees out from under him. He savored her, like long, slow sips from warm, spicy mulled cider. He heard a loud thumping noise, and wondered if it was her heart or his. No, it had to be his. He felt the corresponding vibration in his chest. *This isn't supposed to happen,* he thought. But how could it be anything but good?

Fred raised his head again and stepped back, as if to get out from under a spell radiating down from the mistletoe. Lindsay stared at him numbly. He was backing away. Actually backing away.

"Sorry," he said, glancing up and nodding at the mistletoe over her head. "Just following regulations."

Still dazed, she followed his eyes upward. "And what's the penalty for ignoring mistletoe?"

"Struck by lightning, I think." The familiar smile glimmered at her once again. He made it to the door and turned the knob behind him. "Good night." And he left, with his overcoat still hanging over the back of her sofa. Not that he needed it.

If Lindsay hadn't known better, she would have sworn her nineteenth-century Englishman had just given her a modern American brush-off.

The cold night air did Fred good. But not nearly enough good.

He'd kissed Lindsay with his whole heart, the only way he knew how to do anything. How was he going to let go of her after that? Once he'd had her in his arms, stepping back had felt like tearing off a little piece of his soul. It wasn't just the intoxicating physical sensation. It was the sense of something that was right, something that was meant to be.

But no. He was supposed to spend time with Lindsay, enjoy her company, help her handle her inner demons, all to hand her off to someone else. Someone who'd apparently never even bothered to come after her himself. Not much of a man in Fred's book. Yet he'd been assured that reconciling Lindsay with Steven was in her best interest.

What about *Fred's* best interest?

That was traitorous thinking. Nothing good could come of it.

He had to speak to Headquarters. Have them re-assign him to a nice little old lady who didn't hear from her grandchildren often enough, or something like that.

He continued on his path, just off the sidewalk, listening to his feet crunch in the brittle remains of the snow.

Chapter 8

Dear Wendi,
   Hope this card reaches you before Christmas!
I've been running way behind as usual

Lindsay slapped down the green felt-tip pen with a sigh of disgust. She thought she'd given up on the excuses and apologies, figuring they were just plain tedious to read year after year. Her old friends had to be used to it by now. Just let them think it was dippy Lindsay again.

She didn't feel dippy. She felt jangled into a million pieces.

She should have known she was too keyed up from Fred's abrupt departure to write a cheery Christmas card. But it was too early to go to bed, and she had to pour all this restless energy into *something.*

Lindsay pushed away from the TV tray of cards, heaving herself back against the couch cushions with another exasperated huff. Something fell from the back of the couch and brushed her cheek. Lindsay turned and stared at the sleeve of Fred's overcoat.

It figured. He still had a way to reach her even when he wasn't here.

Tempted to swat the coat away, Lindsay fingered the fabric's warm woolen texture instead. It felt real enough, solid enough. The arms around her had felt solid enough, too. But she'd seen Fred do too many inexplicable things to believe he was just an ordinary man. Yet when push came to shove, he behaved like any of the men Jeanne always complained to her about. He'd gotten her to let her guard down, and then boom, he was gone.

How had she let herself get so worked up? Less than a week ago, she hadn't even wanted to believe he existed. Now she dreaded the thought of Fred going away.

Maybe he already had.

Headquarters looked different.

Then again, it had never *looked* like anything before.

Tonight, Fred arrived to find himself seated in a semblance of an office. It looked a bit like Lindsay's workplace, but it was more—sketchy. He faced a broad, gleaming desk with a single filing cabinet just to the right. Other than that, the room was unfurnished. In fact, it didn't seem to have walls.

The gentleman behind the desk wore a distinguished tweed suit. His dark hair was going gray, but appeared in no hurry to do so. Fred had never seen anyone from Headquarters in physical form before, but still, he would have known his immediate supervisor anywhere.

Fred said the first words that came to mind. "You've redecorated."

The man behind the desk chuckled. "That's something I've always liked about you. Your sense of humor." His British accent matched Fred's. "You've been in the physical world for a while, and you seemed to be having some . . . breathing difficulties the last time you were here. We thought this might make things more comfortable for you."

They'd noticed, then. "Is that unusual?"

An economical shrug. "It happens on occasion. So, what brings you here?" Sitting back cross-legged, the man at the desk appeared relaxed, but his eyes were sharp. From where he sat Fred couldn't tell if they were brown or dark gray.

Fred tried not to squirm in the sumptuous wingback chair. They might decorate on short notice, but they had good taste. "It's about the Lindsay Miller case."

"Naturally."

Naturally. "I'm concerned I may not be the best one for the job."

"And why would that be?" His supervisor spoke with a curious, businesslike empathy.

"I'm afraid I'm getting personally involved."

"My boy, the very nature of our work is personal. It's your personal connection to Miss Miller that makes you able to reach her."

But I wasn't supposed to reach for *her,* he thought. Was it possible his supervisors didn't know about what happened tonight? The graying gentleman in front of him gave no outward indication.

"I'm just not sure I'm up to it," Fred said lamely.

"On the contrary. You're uniquely qualified for this case."

"Why? Because I look like someone you conjured up for her?"

"Of course not. You should know better. You were chosen for her before any of that. The film character was only a convenient image. Just like all this." He gestured at their underfurnished surroundings.

Fred waffled, uncertain how much to say. If they didn't know, he wasn't going to tell them. "I've reached a point where I'm not sure how to proceed."

"That should be simple. It's your job to do what's in her best interest."

Fred pinched the bridge of his nose. He was starting to get one of Lindsay's famous headaches. "I'm not sure what that is anymore."

"You have your instructions."

"To get her to reconcile with Steven." Just to make sure he really understood. It felt so wrong.

"Correct."

His stomach twisted. "Is there any chance her needs have changed?"

"In the past few days? I hardly think so. What could possibly have happened in such a short time?"

He *must* not know what happened tonight, or he'd never ask that question.

Fred took a deep breath. "Is it possible to send a substitute?" The words hurt his throat. But they had to be said. He'd been told who was in Lindsay's best interest, and it wasn't him.

"A substitute?"

"Yes."

"You think that would be best?"

He wanted to scream, *no.*

He wanted more time with Lindsay. For himself— not for any assignment. But that wasn't in her best interest, and time was short. As of tomorrow, Christmas was only four days away.

"Yes," he choked out. "Send someone else." *Preferably in female form.*

His supervisor placed his palms flat on the desk

and stood. He was shorter than Fred expected, but with his dignified, correct posture, an imposing man nonetheless. "We'll try it, Fred. But you have to understand that if it backfires, you accept full responsibility."

"I understand." He blinked. "Wait a minute. You just called me Fred."

His supervisor nodded. "Isn't that the name you've chosen, for the form you've taken?"

The name Lindsay had given him. For a form he would find it extremely difficult to part with.

Lindsay turned in bed, trying to fight her way back up out of sleep. Why was it that no matter how hard it was to fall asleep, you were always sound asleep when you had to wake up? The night had been a long, restless one, and now she was exhausted. At least it was Saturday. She pulled up the sheets, desperately wanting to keep her eyes shut, but a sound reached her ears through the covers.

A light, but demanding, rapping at her front door.

Didn't Fred know about Saturdays?

A blush washed over her as she remembered last night's kiss and his hasty exit. The same memory that had kept her tossing half the night.

With that thought, the last traces of sleep vanished. She sat up, swung her feet to the floor, and found her robe at the foot of the bed. She wrapped it around herself, wondering if Fred knew about bed-head. She raked her fingers through her hair, trying to straighten the mass of morning knots. She should run a comb through it.

Let him wait, she thought.

But the gentle rapping persisted, and she needed to know what he had to say for himself after last night. Lindsay slid her feet into the slippers at the foot of her bed and scuffed her way to the front door.

When she opened it, a silvery-haired gentleman stood before her in the cold morning air, dressed in a conservative gray suit. He held a white paper bag and a steaming Styrofoam cup. "Miss Lindsay Miller?"

His British accent brought a sense of déjà vu. *This is where I came in.* Or maybe he was just a deliveryman. A very distinguished deliveryman.

"Yes?" The crisp air made her shiver.

"We haven't met," he said unnecessarily. "Fred sent me from Headquarters."

Lindsay's hand tightened on the doorknob. "Where is he?"

"I'll explain in a moment. May I come in?"

She'd accepted a lot of things in the past few days, but she wasn't letting another British stranger into her home so easily. For all she knew, he was a kidnapper. Or an international jewel thief.

But deep down, she knew better.

Still, Lindsay held her ground, folding her arms against the freezing air. "How do I know who you are?"

He sighed with a slight smile. "My. You are a suspicious one, aren't you? I suppose I can't blame you." His eyes, the same dark gray as his suit, were kindly. Maybe even paternal, in a distant, uppercrust sort of way. "But Fred wanted me to see you, and I'd appreciate it if you could give me a few moments of your time."

She shouldn't back down. But it was that, or keep standing in the arctic blast coming into her apartment. He was too genteel for her to slam the door in his face. And based on her previous experience, it wouldn't do any good anyway.

Lindsay finally stepped aside and let him in, relieved, at least, to close the door against the cold. She hugged her robe around her. "What's going on?"

Her visitor held the white bag and cup aloft. "I brought breakfast. I believe you're fond of poppy-seed bagels?"

Her stomach lurched. *All* of them knew about her. She never should have let him in.

"I'm not hungry," she said.

"I'm terribly sorry. Would you mind if I set these down?" He nodded across the apartment toward the kitchen table.

"*Where's Fred?*"

He studied her a moment, then crossed the apartment to set the bagels on the table. He turned back toward her, looking slightly awkward for the first time.

"Fred felt someone else might be better qualified for your case," he said.

"So he sent me—what, an understudy?"

"Miss Miller, I assure you, he's very concerned about your welfare."

"You can't be serious. He *quit?* And that's all the explanation I get?"

"That's all the explanation he gave me. But he was very concerned about not losing any of the progress you've made."

"*Progress?*" She couldn't believe her ears. She was a *case,* and he didn't want to lose her *progress.*

"Look," she said, "I was doing fine before you guys showed up."

In the back of her mind she remembered Fred's pleasant voice saying, *Liar.*

She ignored it. "If he—if you—think you can just pick up where he left off—"

Lindsay felt her face heat, remembering exactly where Fred had left off last night. If the older gentleman noticed, he showed no reaction. In fact, he hadn't moved since she started her tirade. He regarded her silently, his hands in the pockets of his slacks, underneath his jacket. The stance reminded

141

her somehow of Fred, and she wondered if they could be related. Did they have relatives in "Headquarters"?

She shook her rambling thoughts aside. "You can tell Fred for me, if he thinks you people can just trot out any old Englishman—"

"If the British accent doesn't suit you, perhaps—"

"*No!*"

Lindsay strode to the front door. "If I'm not worth his time . . ."

She yanked the door open. "Then . . . *bah, humbug!*"

Chapter 9

An hour later, Lindsay whipped the fudge in the pot on the stove, much more vigorously than she needed to. This should be her smoothest batch ever. Her arm would be sore, and she didn't even know whom she was going to give the fudge to this time.

It was nearly noon. She should be shopping. She should be writing cards. But she needed a mindless activity. Any Christmas card she tried to write would probably end up sounding incoherent, anyway. Maybe she should go in for a CAT scan after all. Things like this just didn't happen, not to normal people. Not to sane people.

Her strange visitor started her wondering, all over again, just how much she might have been hallucinating for the past several days. If Jeanne, her bosses and her other co-workers hadn't seen Fred and talked about him afterward, she'd be convinced she needed to have her head examined.

If she *wasn't* crazy, and the older man had told the truth, Fred had sent him. All to avoid facing the woman he'd kissed under the mistletoe last night. She'd heard of men having issues with commitment, but this was ridiculous. By his own account, he'd be gone after Christmas. Couldn't he even deal with her that long?

Lindsay bent her knees, bringing her eyes level with the candy thermometer: 238 degrees. Bingo. She turned off the burner and poured the steaming chocolate mixture into the baking dish on the counter.

It couldn't cool off soon enough to suit her. With a sinking heart, Lindsay knew where most of this fudge would be going. Right onto her hips. In the meantime, she contented herself with licking the spoon. Then scraping out the rest from the edges of the pot.

The doorbell rang. Her heart jumped down into her stomach, then popped back up all the way into her throat.

She shouldn't answer it. She couldn't *not* answer it.

Lindsay crossed the apartment to the front door, half-formed prayers jumbling through her mind, and opened the door. Let it be another kid selling candy bars, or magazine subscriptions. She'd even be glad to see an obnoxious adult, offering her a carpet cleaning demonstration, before she'd be willing to deal with—

Fred stood on her porch with a potted red poinsettia plant in hand and an apologetic look on his face. That expression would have melted the hardest heart, but Lindsay told herself she was numb.

She stood stock still, one hand still firmly gripping the doorknob. "So you couldn't find another errand boy?"

"I'm sorry." He looked sincere, but then, when didn't he?

"'Sorry' doesn't cover it."

"Lindsay." He held the plant out between them, and like a sucker she automatically reached out and took it. Once her hands were full, Fred took the opportunity to nudge the door open and step inside.

"Wait." She turned to follow him, another mistake; he closed the door. "I didn't say you could come in."

"Here, let me take that for you." Fred set the plant on the end table where the horrible fake tree had stood before Fred brought her the real one.

Stay numb, stay cool. "Fred, you can't just barge in here. I've had enough."

"I know." His voice was composed. "I owe you an apology."

She'd expected him to protest his innocence. "So you know about the man who was here this morning?"

"Yes."

"And you really sent him?"

145

"Yes." His eyes fixed on hers, unflinching. "I can explain."

"Explain?" Okay, she wasn't numb anymore. She was furious. "How can I trust you? What is this, a game?"

"No."

She drew in a deep breath to steel herself. To bring all her anger and frustration into focus. "You sent someone else to do your dirty work. One kiss and you run for the hills. *Why?* It's not like you'll even be around a week from now. Of all the cowardly—"

Cowardly. Lindsay stopped short. She had no right to use the word. She'd played it over and over again in her mind, after Steven. Except that, back then, she'd been the coward. Fred didn't know that. Or did he? Was this whole setup his clever little way of getting her to admit what she'd done?

He stood, holding her gaze steadily, waiting for her to go on. If this was a trap, she wouldn't take the bait. Lindsay steered back to the real point at hand. "You *left* me."

"I'm sorry." The gentleness in his eyes, in his voice, was maddening. "Have you been left before?"

"You ought to know."

"No, I don't. I told you, need-to-know basis."

"I'm not buying this need-to-know stuff anymore."

"It's the truth."

How could one single, soft-spoken statement

146

make her want to believe him so completely? Lindsay tightened her jaw. "If this is all some way to get me to tell you about Steven—"

"Lindsay, believe me. Steven is the last person I want to talk about right now."

There was something so utterly convincing in his voice, this time Lindsay didn't doubt him for a moment.

Fred reached up toward her cheek, eyes suddenly filled with quiet purpose, and Lindsay realized he'd been waiting for her to finish. Waiting his turn. He'd seemed so collected. Now, looking up into his eyes, she felt face-to-face with something fathomless, and she couldn't imagine why she hadn't seen it before. No one had ever, in all her life, looked at her that way. Not Steven. Certainly no one in her family. As if she were something incredibly valuable.

Lindsay stepped back before his hand reached her cheek. Because if he touched her, she'd had it. She'd give in.

She whispered, with what little air she could find in her lungs: "What's going on?"

Fred didn't advance toward her. But that heady look didn't diminish. "Are you ready to listen? I know you're upset. But we don't have much time."

Lindsay swallowed hard and took another step back, then realized she'd centered herself almost perfectly under the mistletoe. She shifted slightly, unwilling to back up again.

When she didn't answer him, Fred spoke. "Lindsay, I wouldn't hurt you for the world. Not intentionally. But I was afraid I might be doing you more harm than good. That's why I asked them to send someone else. Last night, before I left"—he glanced up at the mistletoe, still dangling near her head— "you must admit, that wasn't exactly in the script."

"Script?" She tried to dredge up what remained of her anger, but could only manage bewilderment. "You have a *script* on me?"

He sighed, for the first time looking faintly exasperated himself. "Only a figure of speech. Don't you Americans know what a figure of speech is?"

"I thought you weren't British. Or American or anything else."

"I'm not." He shook his head. "I think I've been in this body too long. I'm going native. I'm even starting to get your blasted headaches." He pinched the bridge of his nose. "No wonder Dickens had his spirits do it all in one night."

"*A Christmas Carol* . . . isn't that just—"

"A story. Written by an Englishman, I might add. A very insightful Englishman. But just a story."

She shook her head. Amazing that, for once, he had a headache and she didn't. "I don't know what's real anymore. How can I ever be sure you're telling me the truth?"

"You only have my word, Lindsay." He glanced up at the mistletoe. "Of course, I know of one way to give you more definitive proof."

He stepped closer, within easy reach of her again. "Do you want me to tell you what's real?"

Her heart pounded. "I don't know."

"Lindsay." Would he stop saying her name, or at least stop making it sound like music? "It's December twenty-first. How it got to be December twenty-first, I'll never know."

"Welcome to my world. That's how I feel every year."

"The point is, our time is limited. We lost a morning. A whole morning. Now we can spend our time arguing, or make the most of the time we've got left."

Lindsay's breath caught in her throat as the full meaning of what he was saying reached her. In a few days, he'd be gone. Gone for good.

Fred's tone lightened. "And if I'm not mistaken, you've been cooking fudge again. Maybe you'll even share some with me this time."

That was pure Fred. But—"Why did you come back?"

"I have you to thank for that. You sent my substitute packing. I'm so glad you did."

He took her hands in his, and Lindsay felt literally caught, as though that warm, light hold could keep her from getting away. But this was no spell from the outside. She didn't *want* to move.

"They keep insisting I'm the best one for the job," Fred said. "I'm tired of arguing about it. Especially when being with you is the only thing I want."

149

"Do they know about—" Lindsay flicked a glance up at the mistletoe.

"They must not, or they never would have let me come back here. I know *I* wouldn't trust me alone with you."

Something new glinted behind his eyes. Lindsay tried to decipher it. He looked both as lighthearted and as serious as she'd ever seen him.

"If they're foolish enough to trust me anywhere near you," he said, "they deserve whatever they get." It sounded almost like a vow. "All I know is that I'm where I want to be, for as long as it lasts. And there are only four days left until Christmas."

Her voice quavered. "Four days is nothing."

"No, Lindsay." The lighthearted look fled from his eyes. "It's everything."

He laid the outside of one finger against her cheek, just beside her lips. Lindsay held absolutely still.

"Now," he said, "if you don't mind, I'd like to give you some of that proof."

"But what about—"

His mouth captured hers, silencing the name neither of them wanted to hear.

When Fred finally brought himself to raise his lips from Lindsay's, he cupped her face in his hands and looked down into her eyes.

What a fool he'd been to even think about

handing her over to someone else. This beautiful, fragile, radiant mass of contradictions. Thank heavens she'd sent his supervisor packing, and that they'd allowed him to return. He realized that must have been the outcome he'd hoped for, deep down, all along.

Fred caressed the corner of her mouth with his thumb. Even if he could only have four more days with her, how could he ever have walked away from that? He'd nearly let a treasure slip through his fingers.

Surely no one else could know her the way he did. They'd just met a few days ago, and he felt as if he'd known her forever. Yet there was so much still to learn. The information he'd been given by Headquarters suddenly seemed like nothing, the vaguest pencil sketch, a dull gray list of facts and figures. To know Lindsay was to spend time with her, experience moments with her, to hear her thoughts, memories and wishes from her own lips. If he could manage to refrain from spending all of that time kissing them.

Four more days. How could there ever be time enough? How should he even begin?

The same way he'd gone about everything in his life up to now, Fred decided.

One minute at a time.

* * *

Twenty-four hours later, Lindsay's apartment practically exploded with Christmas cheer, to Fred's great personal satisfaction.

The shopping was done, the presents wrapped and under the tree, waiting to be delivered to co-workers and family. It had snowed overnight, and Fred had drawn back the curtains on the window behind the tree to take advantage of the brilliant white scene outside. Carols sang from the stereo. He'd prodded Lindsay into getting more holiday decorations out of the closet, and lengths of holly garland draped across the top of the television set, the kitchen cabinets, and the mantel above the little fireplace. From the garland on the mantel, they'd hung some of the stray ornaments they hadn't been able to fit on the tree.

Best of all, she remembered a nativity scene in a box on the top closet shelf. Fred promptly evicted the poinsettia plant from the end table next to the sofa and helped her set up the age-old scene.

"Much better." He stepped back and viewed the nativity scene with approval. "What happened to the little electric tree, by the way?"

"I put it in the bedroom. It's not the greatest Christmas tree, but it makes a nice night-light."

He nodded. "There should be a little Christmas in every room in the house. Of course, there's always room for more."

A funny sort of half-smile stole across Lindsay's

face. Smug? Sheepish? He should know by now, but he couldn't tell.

She vanished into the bedroom and returned with a cardboard box, at least as large as the one from the back of the hall closet. Fred hastened to take the load from her hands and carry it the rest of the way into the living room. Lindsay opened the flaps to reveal a small treasure trove of assorted Christmas knickknacks—reindeer figurines, stuffed snowmen, wooden nutcrackers, and more. Some of them were still sealed in their boxes. That was his Lindsay. Still keeping things boxed up. Except that this time, she'd brought them out on her own.

Fred discovered an artificial plastic ball of mistletoe. When Lindsay wasn't looking, he hung it over the kitchen doorway and waited for her to find it.

If she didn't, pretty soon, he'd help.

By late afternoon, they'd found a place for all of it, and Fred nudged the box into the hallway. "Well," he said, "is that everything, Miss Miller? Or are you about to start pulling tinsel out of your ears?"

She laughed. "One strand at a time."

He loved making her laugh. It was a delightful sound—light, abandoned, almost girlish. Nothing like the serious young woman she tried so hard to be.

That had become his strategy. Keep her laughing. Keep her busy. Keep her mind off the stack of

Christmas cards perched mutely on the tray in front of the sofa. The stack had gotten a bit smaller since the night he met her, but the tray itself had never moved. When Lindsay happened to glance at it, her eyes would cloud momentarily. But she was getting good at avoiding looking in that direction.

They were both getting good at avoiding certain things. Like any mention of his orders from Headquarters. Or what came next, when he had to leave her.

For now, her light gray eyes were filled with that sparkle he couldn't get enough of. Somewhere during their little battle underneath the mistletoe, it appeared, she'd decided to trust him, to accept things for what they were at the moment. And he'd do anything in his power to keep it that way. Never mind what Headquarters wanted . . . at least not for now.

"How did you ever get so many decorations?" he asked.

She stood in the center of the living room, surveying their handiwork. "I buy some every year, when they go on sale after Christmas." Her voice dropped. "When I start telling myself that next year is going to be different."

"Well, that's going to stop."

The sparkle dimmed a little. She didn't answer.

"Lindsay," he persisted, "this isn't just my doing. I'm not the one who bought two dozen little reindeer figurines. Even Saint Nick only needs eight. You've wanted this. It's yours. Enjoy it."

"Next year won't be the same." She left the rest unsaid.

So they were in for a bit of seriousness after all. Fred went to her, put one arm loosely around her waist. "No, it won't be the same. It never is. People come and go, they get older, move, have children. There's only one constant in all of Christmas." He nodded toward the nativity scene a few feet away. "And that's reason enough to rejoice."

He watched Lindsay as her eyes followed the direction of his nod. "I know."

If he could leave her with only one thing, it should be that. He shouldn't let his own selfish motives get in the way. But Lindsay looked solemn, and Fred felt a desperate need to lighten the mood.

He knew just how to do it.

"Let's see if we can finish what's left of that fudge." Fred laced his fingers through hers and led her toward the kitchen.

When he stopped her under the archway, and his mistletoe trap, Lindsay laughed. But not for long. He caught her in a kiss, and her arms came up around him immediately, her lips both yielding and giving. It was several minutes before he could bring himself to raise his head. Until now he'd never focused on anything but the present, but until now he'd never believed the present could be so eternal. Did she feel even a fraction of what he felt? He looked down into Lindsay's face, and her eyes were bright once more, her cheeks flushed.

Yes. At least a fraction.

"I thought you were after the fudge." Lindsay didn't move one centimeter toward the kitchen, didn't stir from his arms.

"I found something sweeter."

When he kissed her again, she leaned back against the side of the archway, as if to savor the luxury of the moment. Her fingers tangled in the hair above the nape of his neck, gathering him nearer. The warmth of her body, so close against his, made everything else seem incredibly far away. Lindsay's hands slid down his back, her body pressing more firmly against his.

Impossible ideas flashed through his mind. It was out of the question. But what *would* happen if he carried Lindsay into the bedroom, with that color-flashing tree in the late afternoon dimness?

There was only one answer to that.

Get them both out of this apartment. Fast.

Chapter 10

"Whose idea was this?" Lindsay tried for a joking tone as she stepped out onto the frozen lake. Anything to conceal the near panic in her voice. Panic was winning.

And the question was rhetorical. Who else but Fred could have gotten her to drive up the mountain for the privilege of hobbling across slippery ice on narrow, precarious skates? Under the metal blades on her feet, the surface felt even slicker than it looked.

Fred squeezed her hands in both of his. "I've got you."

That went without saying. Otherwise, she'd already be in a heap. *Six-year-old kids are doing this,* she reminded herself as one of them swooped by, leaving tiny shavings of ice scattered at her feet. Fred's two black-gloved hands held hers securely as he guided her slowly along the ice, keeping them close to the edge of the lake.

When Fred first suggested it, ice skating had sounded like a fun winter adventure. But roller skates—the normal kind, anyway—had four wheels on each foot to keep you anchored to the earth, instead of tottering like a baby giraffe taking its first steps. The fact that Fred was skating backward, in order to face her, didn't ease her mind. She'd feel a lot better if he could see where he was going.

He smiled down at her, apparently amused by her short, jerky strides. "Have you ever done this before?"

"Once. When I was about twelve. Have you?"

"Not that I recall."

"Then how—"

A teenage boy cut across Fred's path from behind, and Fred deftly sidestepped without looking backward. "I think it's one of those osmosis things."

"You mean ice skating is on a need-to-know basis too?"

Fred wobbled slightly. "Watch out. Don't make me think. Remember, I'm the one who's holding us both up."

He took a longer, seemingly effortless stride backward, and Lindsay felt them pick up a little speed. She jittered off balance, gripping his gloved hands a little more tightly without meaning to. She'd never seen him wear gloves before; she was pretty sure he didn't need the protection from the cold. But they went along with the whole ensemble: the warm overcoat, the bright red scarf—he'd even worn the top hat again tonight, with Lindsay's approval. On the street, it would have been ridiculous, but in this wintry setting, it seemed fine, more flattering than the knit caps or ski masks some of the men out here wore. The top hat was jaunty. It was Christmasy.

Or maybe she'd left her sanity behind before they even left her apartment.

When she didn't totter over, Fred increased their speed again. Lindsay felt a light brush of the cold night air on her cheeks, and started to remember why this had sounded like a good idea.

"Better?" Fred said.

"Better. But would you mind not skating backward?"

"For you, anything." He said it lightly, yet she heard a ring of truth in his voice.

He shifted her right hand to his left and stepped alongside her with an ease that would have surprised her in anyone else. He left the outer edge of the lake to Lindsay, a little extra measure of security. That was something else. Indoor ice rinks had a ledge. Here, there was nothing but Fred to hold on to.

Not a bad deal, she decided, as he tucked her mittened hand into his arm. In fact, she'd be hard-pressed to think of a better one. Lindsay slid on the ice alongside him a little more smoothly now—not graceful by a long shot, but it felt good. It seemed easier now that they faced the same direction.

Fred had been in a pretty big hurry to get them out of the apartment, and it wasn't hard to figure out why. The bracing air was close to the literal equivalent of a cold shower, and Lindsay knew she, for one, had needed it. Out here, under the glare of the outdoor lamps, she could get as close to Fred as she wanted, and not worry about anything getting out of hand.

Even without that, they had to be breaking Headquarters rules six ways from Sunday. But if it didn't bother Fred, she wasn't about to bring it up.

How had she gone from brandishing a walking stick between them, to this?

And how in the world was she going to go back to her normal life after this?

Less than a week ago, she'd been buried in her routine of going to and from work, trying to fulfill her obligations in between, all while she watched Christmas pass her by in a blur from the corner of her eye. Now she was in the heart of it, feeling the bracing air around her, holding a hand she could swear was giving her warmth straight through both of their gloves.

But it was so much more than physical warmth she felt. Fred made her feel special, valued. He made the world around her look better, too: brighter, richer, as if she were seeing it more clearly. Lindsay couldn't remember feeling this way with any other man, not even Steven, and she hadn't gotten that close to anyone else since. With Steven she'd felt safe and comfortable. *Pleasant,* she admitted to herself reluctantly.

Being with Fred was so much better. So much more than she deserved.

And he'd be gone so soon.

Her stride faltered, and Fred's arm instantly boosted her up for support. "Thinking again, weren't you? Remember, the secret of a thing like this is *not* to think."

She wondered if he was talking about the skating, or not.

Fred glided them into a turn as they approached the row of wooden barricades that blocked the unused portion of the lake from skaters—whether for safety, or to keep the public skating area down to a manageable size, Lindsay wasn't sure. But as they crossed the center of the lake, she tried not to think about the depth of the water underneath them.

Not to think. Don't think about the water. Don't think about what happens when he leaves.

And then they reached the shore on the other side, and turned again. Fred's arm squeezed her hand closer against him. And Lindsay's heart lightened, along with her steps. She drew a deep breath of the cold air.

The lake was beautiful. The white ice and snow, the bright sweaters and caps of the skaters around them, all against the distant backdrop of the black night sky, with its tiny white pinpricks of stars. Tinny holiday music played from public address speakers near the skate rental shack, and even that sounded pretty in context. *It's that time of year . . . When the world falls in love . . .*

Her skates slid smoothly along the ice now, and Lindsay felt light inside, almost as if she weren't touching the ground. She had to hand it to Fred. Never had she lived so completely in the present. There was nothing but *now.* Lindsay took it all in, and let the moment fill her heart.

She had no right to be this happy.

Fred guided Lindsay once again around the lake, feeling her relax a bit more with each stride. It was like watching a flower blossom in the snow, seeing her open up this way. And the bud had been beautiful to begin with. Once, he tried to spin them at the shallow part of the lake, near a soft-looking snowbank. They'd nearly tottered over; after she shrieked, she collapsed against him in a spate of that little-girl laughter.

Their Christmas outings certainly seemed to be doing her some good. But at this point, he could no longer pretend he was doing this for anyone but himself. Making Lindsay happy made him happy. A strange form of selfishness, perhaps, but selfishness nevertheless.

And as for that invisible nemesis, Steven—

He drew Lindsay a little closer as they rounded the turn that took them along the blocked area across the center of the lake, the part that made her nervous. Once again her fingers squeezed tighter around his, and he squeezed back.

It couldn't possibly make any difference to Fred whether he sent her back to Steven or not. Either way, come Christmas, Fred would never see her again. Still, something at the very core of him resisted.

Before, he'd never had a *plan*. But he'd always had a *purpose*. This was like being in free fall. Exactly like being in free fall—both exhilarating and terrifying. What repercussions from Headquarters awaited him on the other side of these four days, he didn't know. But in this moment, one thing was crystal clear: he was going to enjoy Lindsay while he had her, and the consequences be damned.

Seconds later a loud, sharp noise filled the air. Followed by a thousand smaller, crackling noises under his feet.

Lindsay heard a sound like a gunshot. An instant later someone yanked her left arm and wrenched her away from Fred. She tried to pull free, to get back to him, but she couldn't even see him. People blurred in front of her as someone dragged her backward by both arms now, the blades of her skates scraping the ice. Huge, spiderwebbing cracks radiated outward across the ice. She heard a referee's whistle, shouting voices, and behind it all, that ominous cracking sound.

A louder shot than before—an explosive one—and an enormous plume of water burst upward, behind the people who blocked her view of Fred.

The last of the crowd in front of her streaked past as people reached the shallow edges of the lake, herded by safety workers in bright red vests. Still straining against the hands that pulled her, Lindsay stared at a jagged, gaping hole in the ice twenty feet away from her.

A tall, black hat floated on top of the water.

Chapter 11

They wouldn't let her get near him. Hands and arms kept pulling her back, she didn't know how many, only that she couldn't get to the hole in the ice that had just swallowed Fred. Lindsay's heart slammed against her ribs like a jackhammer. Gradually she realized she was screaming.

"Calm down," said a husky man on her right. He had her arm locked behind her. She focused on him long enough to see he was one of the dozen or so safety attendants she'd seen scattered around the lake.

Why was he wasting his time holding her back, when he should be helping Fred?

She stopped screaming, not because he said to calm down, but because she was exhausted by the futility of screaming. Her arms ached, and she stopped pulling against the other hands that restrained her. Abruptly she felt limp. She couldn't take her eyes away from that jagged hole, its edges like huge, carnivorous teeth.

How long had it been? Thirty seconds? Three hours?

She turned to her red-vested watchdog. He had a broad, ruddy face. "You need to—"

He put a hand on her shoulder, as if afraid she might go berserk again, and nodded toward a cluster of other red-vested workers on the ice, about midway between the hole and the crowd of skaters.

The scene started to make some kind of sense. With what seemed like agonizing slowness, the safety crew dispersed to form a chain, lying flat and facedown, leading across the precarious cracked ice toward the hole. Each one grasped the legs of the man in front of him—ready, she realized, for a secondary rescue if the ice cracked any further. Lindsay's eyes fixed on the opening again. Could anyone still be alive under there?

Could Fred die? She didn't know.

This is all my fault, all my fault, all my fault, although she couldn't say why, except that if it weren't for her, he wouldn't be here to begin with. Even now, she wasn't doing him any good. She'd been completely useless. Worse than useless— she'd panicked.

A black-gloved hand gripped the ice at the edge of the water.

Lindsay stepped forward without thought, only

to have the attendant take a firmer grip on her shoulder. She watched, helpless, as the first man reached the gloved hand. Slowly, they pulled a limp black figure out of the hole.

The next thing Lindsay knew, the beefy attendant next to her had shoved her head down between her knees, practically knocking her off her feet.

"I'm not going to faint," she said.

"Not now, you're not," he agreed.

She straightened, slowly, still restrained by the rough hand at the back of her neck. To her alarm, they were taking Fred's droopy form *away*, supported by three or four of the men, toward the skate rental shack across the lake from where she stood. "I have to—"

"You have to wait here," he said with exaggerated patience. "The paramedics are on their way. We need to get him dry, check his vital signs . . ."

Vital signs. Lindsay felt the bottom drop out of her stomach. The idea of Fred's flesh-and-blood vulnerability hit her full force once again. Would his body work the same way as anyone else's when they examined him? She had no idea.

It's all my fault. But even her guilt seemed self-centered, so she closed her eyes and directed all her energy, prayers and concentration into one thought: *just let him be all right.*

* * *

Fred remembered very little of what came next. But then, very little of it made sense.

He found himself in some sort of crude back room, all concrete and wood, surrounded by red-vested attendants. They covered him in stale-smelling blankets, checked his pulse, and generally made nuisances of themselves. There was only one thing he needed. Didn't they know that?

"Is Lindsay all right?"

"Who's Lindsay?" one of them said.

Another one said, "She must be the one who was out there screaming her head off."

Fred tried to shove himself upright, and two of them pushed him back down with unnecessary zeal. He fell back on the small, rickety cot like a sack of potatoes. Cold, wet potatoes.

"They're bringing her over here to wait for you," a third one said, and Fred instantly rated him the only useful one of the lot.

Things got hazy after that. They seemed obsessed with making sure his heart and lungs worked. From somewhere, they produced dry clothes for him. That, at least, made sense. His hands and feet were numb at first; then they were on fire, which the men assured him was a good thing. The rest of him was cold, cold in a way he'd never been before. He'd heard the expression, "chilled to the bone," and now he knew exactly what it meant.

Finally, they let Lindsay in. A paler Lindsay than he'd ever seen before. She'd obviously been worried, and for some odd reason her concern was a welcome sight. He tried to think of something clever to say, to show her he was all right. Nothing came.

Lindsay didn't say anything either. Just went to him and draped herself over him in a gentle, protective hug. Her hair fell across his face. It tickled abominably, and nothing had ever felt more wonderful.

There was nothing else he needed.

An hour later, he still couldn't get warm.

Fred huddled on Lindsay's couch, buried under the arsenal of blankets she'd brought out to him. She'd put him at the end of the sofa closest to the fireplace, though she acknowledged that the blue-orange gas flames didn't contribute much in the way of heat.

Not that it mattered. This cold came from inside, probably the way most people would feel after being dunked in sub-freezing water. But he'd never felt any kind of cold, beyond that brisk, tingling feeling at the surface of his skin, or that delicious, bracing air that made him feel energetic.

He'd never even shivered before. Now, he couldn't seem to stop.

And Lindsay couldn't seem to sit down.

She was off in the kitchen, doing what, he wasn't sure. She hadn't stopped searching for ways to make him comfortable since they stepped in the door. When all he really wanted was for her to *land*, preferably somewhere within reach.

Finally he got his wish. Lindsay arrived with a steaming mug in hand—only one—and placed it on a tray she'd set up next to the sofa. She sat beside him, leaning against his arm, and Fred closed his eyes. Even through the layers of blankets, she brought a warmth he could feel.

He wanted to raise his arm and put it around her, but he couldn't quite summon up the energy. And he didn't know if he should.

Things had gone terribly wrong, and he suspected he knew why.

"Drink that," she said. "It should help warm you up."

He'd never been fussed over before either, another new experience. He couldn't decide whether he liked it or not. He did know he'd been pleased, in some perverse way, by the concern he'd seen in Lindsay's face back at the lake, but that seemed wrong. He shouldn't be glad to see her upset for any reason.

So he cooperated, and sipped from the mug she

brought him. It tasted strange and salty, not at all what he'd expected. "What is this?"

"Chicken broth." She started to move. "I'm sorry, can I get you—"

"No. Please." He almost laughed. "Don't get up again. You're the only warm thing in here."

She settled back down, her soft weight returning to lean against his arm. Fred took another cautious sip from his mug, trying to equate the taste and smell with those chicken pieces he'd seen Lindsay eating the other day. Eons ago.

A moment later, her hand reached for his under the blanket. But instead of holding his hand, her fingers traced below his palm and came to rest on the inside of his wrist. Checking his pulse?

He said dryly, "And what is that going to tell you?"

Her fingers went still, and he regretted his tone. "I don't know. I think normal is supposed to be seventy-two or something like that." She slipped her fingers loosely through his. Better. "When they had you back there to check you over, I was afraid they might find a fifth heart or something."

That loosened a chuckle in his chest. It had a strange ache to it; he wasn't sure if the sensation was physical or not. "I hadn't thought of that." All he'd thought about was where Lindsay was, and when they'd bring her to him. "A *fifth* heart?"

Her shoulder shrugged against his arm. "I guess

171

I figured if anyone had an extra heart, it would be you."

Fred stared at the fire. She had no idea what a selfish creature he'd turned out to be. He'd strayed far off the mark of his assignment—her best interest—and thought only of himself. And Headquarters had let him know it, in no uncertain terms. "This was no accident, you know."

Her head lifted away from his shoulder, and he was sorry he'd said it. "What?"

"Think about it. That lake opened up under one person." He smiled slightly. "You and I haven't exactly been playing by the rules, you know."

"You mean—instead of being struck by lightning, they . . . ?"

He shrugged, trying for a lightness he didn't feel. "You have to admit, it was an effective way to get my attention."

In the soft glow of the firelight, her lovely eyes went round and horrified. She released his fingers and sat back, away from him, taking her warmth away with her. "Then it *is* my fault."

What was she talking about? And what was he trying to do to the poor girl? With an effort, he freed his hand from the layers of blankets and reached for hers. "Lindsay. Relax. It's *my* fault. I'm the one who's not doing my job. After all, they didn't drop *you* through the ice."

He wouldn't have thought her eyes could get

any larger, but they did. At last he caught her hand and squeezed it. "Know what? Maybe I could use something else after all. Some hot chocolate?"

He didn't know why he thought that might make her feel better, but it seemed to.

In the kitchen, Lindsay allowed herself a brief moment to rest her elbows on the counter and cover her eyes. She took several deep breaths, keeping them quiet so Fred wouldn't hear.

This isn't about you. Caving in to her own emotions wouldn't do him any good.

He wanted a cup of hot chocolate. This, she could do. Lindsay opened the cabinet by the sink. Ovaltine. Milk. And yes, a dash of vanilla.

A few minutes later she returned to the living room, mug in hand. Lindsay froze and stared, not moving, until the slow movement of his chest reassured her that he was breathing.

It was a sight she'd never seen before, and somehow strangely disquieting.

Fred Holliday was sound asleep on her couch.

Lindsay woke to another unfamiliar sound: a man's cough from down the hall. Her eyes snapped open, and she swung her legs over the bed before her brain could catch up.

Fred, coughing. This couldn't be right.

She hastily grabbed her robe, then stumbled out to the living room. The coughing came again as she headed down the hall, and she tried to assess it with an amateur ear. Maybe not a deep, lung-wracking cough, but it didn't sound good.

All six feet of Fred lay twisted across Lindsay's five-foot couch, and a night's sleep hadn't improved the position she'd clumsily stretched him out into last night. The multiple blankets she'd pulled from the cabinets, and her own bed, knotted around him. His eyes were closed; she couldn't tell if he was awake or not. Gingerly, she rested the outside of her fingers on his cheek. Hot. Of course.

And unshaven. Fred had never needed a shave before.

At her touch, he opened his eyes, his expression glassy at first. One arm came up to encircle her shoulders, pulling her down in a loose sort of hug. He murmured, "Are you my guardian angel?"

A Fred joke, or was he hallucinating as well as feverish? Lindsay straightened to get a better look at him, and his arm slid away with no resistance. There seemed to be no strength in it.

He said, "Something tells me that hot chocolate's gotten cold."

Well, that at least, was lucid. "Eight hours will do that," she said.

"What happened to my coat?"

All right. He definitely wasn't all there. "It got wet."

"I know that, silly. I mean, where is it?"

"Hanging over a chair in the kitchen. I brought in all your clothes last night."

"Oh. I feel different." He glanced down at the navy blue sweatshirt he wore, with sleeves that barely reached his wrists. His change of clothes had been cobbled together last night from well-meaning bystanders. Everyday, wrong-fitting, contemporary street clothes must feel very strange to him.

Fred started to speak again, but bent forward instead under the force of another spate of coughing.

Too big to fit on her sofa, yet he seemed helpless. Lindsay rested a hand lightly on the back of his shoulder, wincing as she felt his body shake. She was discovering she had some alarming latent nurturing instincts. But no idea how to use them. "You're sick," she said.

"I noticed." Fred slumped back down onto his pillow with a wry smile. "Don't worry. I'm sure it's nothing more serious than the common cold."

She frowned. "You're not supposed to get those."

"It's all right." His voice didn't have its usual resonance.

She went with the basics. "Are you hungry?"

175

"I think so." Fred looked as though the idea were new to him. It probably was. She'd seen him eat things like chocolate, chestnuts and hot cocoa, but never a meal. She started to get up, and he blinked. "Lindsay, I can't have you—"

She stood and folded her arms, looking down at him from her new dominant height. She couldn't help cracking a smile. "Try and stop me."

Scrambled eggs, she decided. Nourishing, but not too challenging to eat. Breaking the eggs into the skillet, Lindsay took comfort in being able to do something useful. How traditional. Just a woman cooking breakfast for—

She looked toward the doorway leading into the living room. If Fred wasn't an angel, what *was* he? And why was he suddenly so very, very human?

Her heart sank at the sound of more coughing from the next room. *I did this.* She brushed the useless thought away and concentrated on making breakfast. Dim gray light filtered in through the kitchen window, reminding her of another reality: it was Monday morning. She was supposed to go to work. Her last day and a half of work before she went on vacation. Calling in wouldn't look good. But she didn't like the thought of leaving Fred in this condition. In fact, something primal inside her felt very uneasy about leaving him alone now.

* * *

Fred started awake at a sound next to him, and opened his eyes to see Lindsay setting a plate and glass on the tray he'd been using last night. Good grief, had he been asleep again?

Sitting up, even halfway, was an incredible effort. He felt abominably weak. He picked experimentally at the scrambled eggs. Unless you counted the chicken broth Lindsay foisted on him last night, he'd never eaten food for nourishment before. If it wasn't sweet or otherwise delicious, there hadn't seemed to be any point to it. But he had a feeling he needed to now.

He saw Lindsay glance furtively at the little pendulum clock that hung across the room. "You need to go to work today, don't you?"

"I'm supposed to. But . . ."

Did he really seem that feeble? Getting her off work early for a Christmas excursion was one thing. Keeping her home because he was a helpless heap on her couch was unacceptable. "Don't be ridiculous. You can't stay home on my account. It's not as if I'm going to evaporate without you."

Her face paled, and Fred realized that was exactly what she was afraid of. He never should have made those jokes about being struck by lightning or vanishing in a puff of smoke.

He tried logic. "Lindsay, if Headquarters was going to be that vicious, I never would have come back up through the ice. They don't *do* things like that. Trust me."

He was ninety percent certain he was telling the truth.

"Then why are you sick?"

"That, I'm not sure. I still need to sort it out." He tried for Gruff, Irritable Male. "Maybe if I had some time alone—"

He couldn't tell if Lindsay saw through it or not. She hesitated, one hand clutched through her hair, something he hadn't seen her do in a while. She left the room and returned a moment later with a small white stick. A thermometer, he realized.

"Now, I ask you again, what's that going to tell you? For all you know my normal temperature is—"

She inserted it under his tongue, shutting him up effectively. There didn't seem to be much point in resisting. For all her uncertainties, Lindsay had an undeniable core of determination.

A few minutes later, it beeped. She pulled it out, examined it, and frowned. "A hundred."

"What does that mean?"

"It's not too bad." She clicked the thermometer against her thumbnail, obviously still at war with herself. She looked at Fred again. "I'd still feel better—"

"Lindsay, *go*."

Eventually she did. But not before she gave him a complete rundown on the contents of the refrigerator, cleared his dishes, urged him to drink fluids, and showed him how the remote control on the television set worked. Now that she was leaving him on his own, she'd reverted from firm and in-charge to fretting and fluttering.

What did she think—he wouldn't die if she was watching?

Wisely, this time, he didn't say it out loud.

Lindsay closed the door behind her, and he missed her immediately. Fred rested his head on the pillow, marveling that anyone could be so exasperating and so wonderful at the same time. It all seemed to be tied up in the same feeling, one he didn't dare put a name to.

Soon, though, that strange, drifting sensation started to claim him. It was odd, this need for rest. Usually either he was awake, or he simply—*wasn't*. Being where he wanted to be was a simple matter of thinking it, and it was so. In between, there was nothing. Instead of all this meaningless time, drifting in and out of awareness, while the hours slowly crept.

Apparently this body, in its current condition, needed sleep to fight whatever illness this was. His head ached, and his chest felt cramped and heavy. All right, Headquarters was giving him a little taste of mortality. Very amusing. He wondered if they realized mortality wouldn't be so bad, if Lindsay came along with it. But that wasn't the plan they'd set before him. They were reminding him of that now, in no uncertain terms.

What they hadn't done, as of now, was allow him to contact them. After the first few hours, he got tired of trying to will himself there to report in. Obviously, they'd left him to sort it out on his own.

He reached for the remote control. Fred fixed his eyes on the colored screen, trying to distract himself with the images. He couldn't be sure, but it seemed part of the purpose of television was *not* to think. He paused at a channel showing something in black, white and gray. It was a welcome respite, more soothing to his eyes than all that garish color.

In a moment he recognized the show. It was Lindsay's movie, *A Christmas Carol*. He knew the story backward and forward because Lindsay loved it, but he wasn't really familiar with the film. He'd barely given it a second glance the first night he came to Lindsay's apartment. Now, he saw himself walk into Ebeneezer Scrooge's little office.

Oh, this was strange.

Thanks to his inherent, need-to-know familiarity with the story, he could practically recite the dialogue by heart. But he was transfixed by the image of himself, this cheery Fred who knew all the answers.

Had that really been him, a week ago? Or had that certainty started to falter from the very first time he set eyes on a vulnerable, fair-haired girl?

He drifted again, and when he opened his eyes, the television was in color again, blaring out an obnoxious commercial for last-minute holiday savings.

Chapter 12

Lindsay hurried home as quickly as she could, half-convinced Fred wouldn't be there by the time she got back. The words *I killed an angel* kept running through her head all day. This never would have happened to him if it hadn't been for her.

He denied being an angel. But he'd never been anything but kind to her, and for the life of her, Lindsay couldn't think of any good she'd ever done him. If he wasn't an angel, what was he?

The front doorstep was dark when she put her key in the lock. December twenty-third, one of the shortest days of the year. No lights from her tree glowed through the curtains of the front window; she should have turned the tree on for Fred. If he'd been able-bodied at all, surely he would have turned the tree lights on himself.

If he was still there.

With that last thought, she shouldered her way into the apartment, afraid of what she'd find.

She entered quickly enough to see Fred's head jerk as he started awake. He still lay slumped on the couch, very similar to the position she'd left him in this morning, his head raised slightly from propping the pillow on the arm of the couch.

He blinked at her sudden entrance. "Yes? The fire is in the apartment two doors down."

Alive, awake, and a joke. She couldn't have hoped for better. Lindsay leaned against the doorjamb, smiling as relief flooded her limbs. Then she thought of all the cold air she was letting in, and shut the door. "I didn't mean to wake you up."

"Don't apologize. You're a breath of fresh air. Literally."

He still didn't sound like himself. Lindsay crossed the room to him, trying to assess whether he seemed any better. He looked pale under the single overhead living-room light. Had he eaten? She wondered if he'd made it off the couch at all today.

She put a hand to Fred's forehead. To her surprise, he moved it away, then held on to it and studied it as if he wasn't sure what to do with it. "Sorry," he said, to her hand. "I'm still not used to that."

"To what?"

"Being the one someone else takes care of. I like it and I don't."

"Well, you'd better learn to like it. Because you don't have a choice."

He smiled, as though admitting defeat, and finally met her eyes again. Something was missing, in his eyes or in his smile, and Lindsay wondered fleetingly if they'd sent her a different Fred again. But no, she didn't think so. This felt like her Fred—just with something subtracted. Was it the illness, or something else? She put her hand to his forehead, and this time he let her. Still warm. But probably no warmer than this morning, and she hadn't heard him cough since she walked in.

She tried to put her unease aside, and heated up some soup. Then ate some herself, when Fred insisted. She sat at the far end of the couch, doing her best not to crowd his legs, or to notice the growing silence between them as they ate. The silence lasted while Lindsay cleared away their bowls and trays.

When she returned, Fred still sat upright on the couch, although his limbs hung more loosely than usual. Maybe the fraction of a bowl of soup he'd finished had done him some good. He spoke before she reached him. "We need to talk."

He sounded better, more like himself, but something still felt wrong. Lindsay hovered halfway across the living room, suddenly reluctant to take a seat.

I'm not going to like this.

Fred rested a hand on the sofa cushion next to him. "Come sit down."

The brown velour cushion looked as inviting as an electric chair. Lindsay approached it warily and sat, growing more alarmed when Fred took her hand in both of his. She would have thought he was about to tell her her cat had died, if he hadn't already died two years ago.

He didn't speak until she met his eyes, dark and searching. Lindsay's fingers curled inward until the gentle pressure of Fred's hands stilled them. "I had a chance to do some thinking today." He nodded toward the television set. "When the only alternative is looking at that bloody thing, you find you have a lot of time to think."

She didn't laugh.

"Lindsay, I've tried walking around and around it. It's amazing how long you can ignore the obvious if you really want to. I've been terribly selfish. I've been told what's best for you, and I've willfully shut my eyes to it."

He'd been selfish? Angel or not, the man was insane.

"It's pretty obvious neither of us have been in any hurry to get you back to Steven. I think we both know why. At least I know my reasons. Why don't you tell me yours?" Fred squeezed her hand gently, holding it between both of his as surely as his eyes held hers. Eyes that only seemed to see the good in her. They'd always looked at her with such warmth, warmth she'd come to depend on, without even knowing when it happened.

"Help me do my job," he said. "Tell me about Steven."

"I can't." She couldn't pull away from that steady gaze, but she tried to pull her hand back.

Fred held it, with more firmness than he could have managed this morning. "Why?"

Because if I do you'll never look at me that way again. "I just can't."

"Lindsay, it's one step. It doesn't obligate you to take any others. But if we don't move forward, we can't hope to change things." A smile quirked at the corner of his mouth. "And you'll be stuck here with a sickly Englishman on your couch."

She could think of worse things. Like exposing the weakest, ugliest part of herself. But she knew there was more at stake than her petty personal issues. This Headquarters wasn't going to let Fred exist on her couch forever. For all she knew, he'd wither away.

His dark brown eyes stayed on hers. Lindsay felt the urge to draw something up around her for protection, like one of the blankets twisted at the far end of the couch. But preferably something stronger. Steel, perhaps.

She took a deep breath. "It's not a nice story."

"Try me."

Lindsay wrenched her eyes away from his, concentrating instead on the large, blank eye of the television screen straight ahead. "It's like I told you. We dated all through high school. I think everyone always figured we'd end up together. Maybe I did too, I don't know. But when I finished high school, I went to college in Denver. Four hours away. Steven stayed home and went to the community college. We didn't make any plans. . . ." Lindsay squirmed out of her shoes and drew her feet up onto the couch, hugging her knees. "I think I kind of liked the fact that Denver was four hours away. I wasn't half of a couple there. People didn't look at me and see Steven's girlfriend. We'd been together so long, I guess I wanted to find out who I was on my own."

She stared at the darkened gray screen. Her reflection looked small and huddled. Cowardly. Beside her, Fred didn't make a sound. She didn't risk a glance in his direction. If she was lucky maybe he'd fallen asleep again.

"We didn't see each other again until I came home for Christmas break." Even the sight of her reflection on the gray glass was too much to bear. She switched her gaze to the fabric of her slacks, trying to lose herself in the individual threads. "On Christmas, he gave me a present. A diamond ring."

She tightened her arms around her knees. The

urge to curl into a ball was nearly insurmountable. *Why are you making me do this?* "I couldn't say anything. So I didn't. I couldn't even look at him. I just hugged him. And we were engaged." She rested her head on her knees and closed her eyes. "For about a week."

She felt a light hand at her back—Fred's—and flinched, shaking it off. "I've always wondered if he thought something was wrong with me that week. I spent a lot of time holed up at home. I said I had a big term paper due when I got back to school."

Lindsay forced her voice past the ache in her throat. "I was already packed to go back the day before New Year's. Steven gave me a call, said he was having a little New Year's Eve party at his house. . . ." She took a deep breath. "When I got there, it was a big surprise party. For me. For us. Balloons, streamers. Everybody jumped out and yelled when I walked in—I just stood there with my mouth open. He must have worked so hard on it."

She closed her eyes. "Then Steven came up and gave me a kiss, and he announced our engagement. I'm sure everybody knew, but—well, he wanted to celebrate. I smiled as big as I could, and I felt like the heel of the universe. I kept thinking, *This isn't how I'm supposed to feel.* I just wanted to run away.

"So, later on, when no one was looking—I did."

Lindsay willed herself to breathe slowly. "I went

into Steven's room and left the ring on his dresser. And I sneaked out." She pressed her forehead hard against her knees and kept her eyes shut tight. "I didn't even leave a note. I didn't know what to say. When I went home, my parents were already in bed, so I grabbed my bags and drove back to Denver that night."

She still couldn't look at Fred. He'd seen something special in her, or at least thought he had. Now he knew better.

"That's it," she said.

Silence stretched out. Lindsay finally opened her eyes. A tear fell on her slacks, but they were black. It didn't show.

"So," he said softly, "you're the one who did the hurting. It never crossed my mind. I didn't think you could hurt anybody."

Another silence, and Fred's fingers brushed her temple. He tucked a section of hair behind her ear, as though searching for a better look at her face. She turned away.

"Lindsay," he said, "it's not the end of the world."

His tone was gentle. Lindsay blinked hard and turned around to look at him. Fred studied her, his features contemplative, but not quite as if a singularly ugly worm had just crawled out from under a rock.

"You don't think I'm horrible?" It seemed like such a childish thing to say, but she couldn't help it.

He gave her a wry grin. "Well, for one thing, you didn't do it to *me*. For another, you were eighteen years old."

"Nineteen."

"Oh. You're a monster, then."

Lindsay let out a laugh that was half a sob. "You're not helping." She leaned her elbows on her knees and rested her forehead against her palms. "It's the worst thing I ever did."

Fred rested a hand lightly on the nape of her neck. "Why *did* you do it?"

"I didn't want to face him."

"That goes without saying. But why didn't you want to marry him?"

All those years ago, she hadn't known how to explain it to Steven. Now, it had been so long since she thought about it, Lindsay wasn't sure she could explain it to herself, or to Fred. "I didn't know what I wanted," she said slowly. "I'd never even dated anyone else. Not since I was fourteen. I guess I didn't expect him to . . ." She shrugged helplessly.

"And you never heard from him again?"

Lindsay shook her head.

"Interesting," he said. Interesting?

His fingers curled loosely in the hair at the nape of her neck, lingering for a moment before he took his hand away. The back of her neck felt colder.

"All right," he said. "Let's take a look at this. My

guess is, you've spent so much time just feeling guilty, it's been a long time since you thought about how you really felt about Steven. Am I right?"

"I guess so."

"And maybe, when you were nineteen, your expectations just weren't realistic. You weren't ready. And maybe now you are."

Lindsay turned to stare at Fred, in his slightly undersize sweatshirt, his features so calm and composed. Her insides clenched. Why? What was he saying that was different from what he'd said all along? She'd been shrinking back from it, avoiding it, since the day he'd first told her she was supposed to be reconciled with Steven. Why should she be surprised to hear it now?

Still, she shook her head. "You can't be serious."

"Of course I am. Don't you see? It's all starting to make sense now. You made a mistake ten years ago. And I'm trying to tell you it's not such a terrible thing."

So helpful, so supportive, so neutral, so objective. Just a man doing his job. Was this the same man who'd kissed her? It couldn't be. Where had he gone?

"The incredible thing is," Fred said, "you're being given the chance to put it right."

Incredible? Lindsay stared into the calm dark eyes and felt something fall out from under her. A hurt started up that felt like ground glass in her stomach. It hurt worse than telling him about Steven, though she wouldn't have thought that was possible.

She whispered, "You really want me to do this? Go back to him?"

Fred's expression didn't change. "I want what's best for you. That's the only reason I'm here."

The only reason. It was true. He was here to do his job. Everything else had been a lie.

"Did you love him?" He asked the question with the same implacable expression.

"Yes." It was true. But it wasn't the whole truth.

And she saw it. Or thought she saw it. A sharp flicker of pain in Fred's eyes, and Lindsay realized with shame that she'd wanted to put it there.

The flicker vanished. "Then that's where you belong."

"No." The word came out without her meaning it to, and Lindsay gave up the one weapon she might have had. "It was nothing like—" . . . *the way I feel about you.* She couldn't even say it. It was too humiliating. And she knew Fred didn't want to hear it.

"Lindsay, you and I—you need to forget it. None of this was supposed to happen."

"You mean, not in the script." Her words came out dead and dull.

"That's right." A timbre that had been missing from his voice since he fell through the ice had returned. *He's getting better,* she realized. Better, because he was back to doing his job.

She should let him. But suddenly, facing a thousand hurt and resentful Stevens didn't bother her nearly as much as the fact that Fred *wanted* her to do it.

"You set me up." Her voice rasped; she was amazed it worked at all. "None of this was real. It was all just to split me wide open—" Probably right down to Fred's fall through the ice. Until she finally broke down and spilled the truth. To help *him.* What a laugh.

He didn't contradict her.

She clutched at one slim, remaining straw. "You said I didn't have to—"

"No, you don't. I can't *make* you do anything. But if you don't use what you've learned, then I've failed you and all this was for nothing."

Nothing. Lindsay felt as if she were inside a glass jar and he'd just tightened the lid, neatly cutting off all her oxygen. Her eyes blurred so badly that she couldn't even see. Only one thing mattered in that moment. Not to have *him* see her like this. She levered her way off the couch, blindly heading anywhere away from him.

A hand caught hers. "Lindsay, wait."

It was back. The gentle voice she'd known all along, and he pulled her back down to the couch with him. Lindsay crumpled against him, knowing she shouldn't, knowing she was an idiot to make herself vulnerable like this. She buried her face in the crook of his neck and tried to keep her tears silent, crying for a hundred emotions she couldn't even name.

"It's all right, darling. I'm here." His arms wrapped tight around her, strong again. His voice, next to her ear, sounded as husky as hers had a moment ago. "Forgive me. It's all true and it's all a lie."

"I don't understand." Her voice came out muffled, between his neck and the pillow.

Fred let out a deep sigh, and she felt his chest slowly sink down underneath her, but she heard no sign of any rattle or cough. "Headquarters knows what's right for you. I have to believe that. *But.* I want you to listen to me very carefully—" He pulled her back from him, just far enough to cup her face between his hands and look straight into her eyes. "If anyone expects me to spend one more minute pretending to feel good about it, they can bloody well forget it."

He smoothed his thumbs gently across her cheeks, wiping away tears. Lindsay searched his eyes. They remained solidly fixed on hers, and she felt a huge tension drain out of her limbs. She shouldn't feel better—not a lot better, anyway—but some important part of the universe had righted itself. She drew in a deep breath. "But you still want me to go back to Steven?"

"It's not a matter of what I want. I'm not supposed to *want* anything, beyond what's best for you. That's what . . ." He broke off. "That's what caring for someone is all about."

"That doesn't answer my question."

"You mean, do I want you to go back to Steven, personally?" He ran one thumb slowly down her now-dry cheek. "Lindsay, for my part, I'd rather be dragged over carpet tacks and dipped in rubbing alcohol. But what *I* want can't matter."

"It's not what *I* want either. I did a terrible thing, but—"

"Terrible." He considered the word, almost as if he were tasting it. "You hurt someone you cared about. You may *feel* terrible, but I don't think it's exactly a capital crime."

"You don't think maybe they're punishing me for—"

"No, no, no. They don't *do* these things for bad people." Fred shook his head. "Believe it or not, no one is trying to torture you, Lindsay. Least of all me. Headquarters—well, I can't say I've been happy about their methods lately, but they do have your best interest at heart. That's why I have to believe Steven will make you happy in the long run. Regardless of what either of us feels now."

"So you don't want me to go back to him. But you want me to."

A smile touched his lips. "In a manner of speaking."

Lindsay lowered her eyes. The bottom line was still the same. Fred still wanted her to go to Steven. And she still lost Fred. That had been a given all along, but somewhere along the line, the thought had become unbearable.

Fred traced the outer line of her lips with his thumb. "What I want," he said, "is impossible. I'm not your future. I can't be."

He drew her close to him, against the soft, unfamiliar sweatshirt. "And no, I can't make you do it. But if nothing good comes of my being here, then all I've done is hurt you, and it would have been better if I never came."

"Don't say that."

"Just promise me you'll think about it."

"What happens to you if I don't?"

"Nothing for you to concern yourself about."

"I'm serious. You've never answered that question." Lindsay pulled back to look at him again, squirming herself into a pretzel twist. "Fred, where *do* you go after this? Do you go off and show someone the true meaning of Valentine's Day, or April Fool's?"

He chuckled. "I don't think so. The fact is—" He looked away, his eyes drifting past her shoulder. Fred almost never did that. "I probably should have told you this a long time ago. I think you're my first case."

"What do you mean, you *think*?"

"It means, I don't remember anything before they briefed me on you. And then I was on your porch. I never questioned it at first. Remember, it's my nature to live in the present. I suppose I assumed that any other cases were irrelevant. But if you're my first assignment, it might explain how I've made such a hash of things."

Lindsay frowned, trying to sort out the implications of that. "Maybe you just don't remember."

Which meant, he might not remember Lindsay after he was gone. And she might not remember him. The idea was so unthinkable, she didn't dare say it. Then another thought occurred to Lindsay, this one wonderful.

He didn't remember anything before they met. Almost as if he'd literally been made for her.

She ran one finger upward over his cheek, feeling the scratch of whiskers that had never existed before. "Are you sure this isn't some way of . . ."

She stopped. What a self-centered, egotistical thought. "Of what?" He reached up and touched the same rough cheek. "Oh. Getting me ready for a life on earth? No. I'm afraid that's just their way of being humorous. My orders are clear." He took her hand down from his cheek and clasped it in his.

"*You* didn't answer *me* yet. I know facing Steven is hard for you. But promise me you'll think about it."

What had she told herself just a little while ago? About being willing to face an army of Stevens? Lindsay cringed inside. She'd rather join Fred being dragged over the carpet tacks. But if she didn't fulfill his "assignment," she had no way of knowing what would happen to him. Fred still seemed certain that Headquarters was always benevolent. After seeing him fall through the ice, Lindsay wasn't so sure.

"I'll think about it," she said. He seemed to be waiting for more. Lindsay licked her lips. "I promise."

He squeezed her hand. "For tonight, that's all I ask."

It would be a hard promise to keep. Because she knew, if she was going to do Fred any good, she had to do more than *think* about it.

Fred turned and stretched his legs out on the couch, pulling Lindsay up to sit in front of him. He let her lean back against his chest, more than happy to serve as her armchair. After today, he owed her that much and more.

As he cradled her against him, they sat facing the Christmas tree she'd forgotten to turn on. That would never do. Fred held his breath, closed his eyes, and remembered that the biggest secret was not to try too hard. An inaudible *click*, and when he opened his eyes, the tree lights had come on. So, things were back as they should be.

Lindsay's head stirred. "You *are* feeling better."

He heard the faint note of regret in her voice and understood it. How nice it would have been if, in some misguided form of punishment, Headquarters had left him earthbound. But that sort of thinking did no good, and it certainly did nothing to lighten the mood.

Fred circled his arms more closely around her waist and rested his cheek against her hair, just above her ear. "Now, do you remember your lesson in Christmas Tree Appreciation? Watch the lights."

He gazed along with her at the large colored bulbs, waiting for that sense of peace to descend. It didn't work. First, a few adjustments still needed to be made. A moment's concentration, and he willed the lights in the room to gradually dim, then started the music on the stereo. The sound of handbells chimed low in the background. Fred remembered they'd been listening to that disc yesterday, before their ill-advised decision to go skating.

"This is one of your favorites, isn't it?" He knew he'd heard it several times.

"Mm-hmm." Her voice sounded much more relaxed, a welcome thing. "I've played a lot more of my Christmas music this year."

"That's one legacy from me I hope you'll keep.

Remember, Christmas is always best when you take it out of the box."

"Don't say 'legacy.' It sounds like—"

"Just a figure of speech, darling." He rested his cheek on the top of her head and breathed in her soft, indefinable scent.

A few minutes later, the sound of Lindsay's breathing became slow and even, and he knew she'd fallen asleep. Small wonder she was exhausted, after all this. His time here might be short, but he was sure he'd already had enough seriousness to last a lifetime.

Fred wrapped his arms around Lindsay and tried to synchronize his breathing with hers. He had no idea where he went from here, and at the moment, he didn't care. This moment was everything. He could have quite happily existed for an eternity here with her, just like this, gazing at the multicolored lights. In the darkened room, they shone both softer and brighter.

He no longer felt the need for sleep. But even if he stayed wide awake for every breath, the hours would pass, and morning would come.

The heaviness he'd felt in his chest all through the day was gone. In its place, an unfamiliar dull ache began to spread through him, and he knew it was only going to get worse.

He held very still and gazed at the tree, trying not to disturb her.

After some time—it might have been minutes or hours—her head slid down under the growing weight of sleep, then bobbed up again. She drew in a sharp little breath, and her body stiffened. Then, with groggy, sluggish movements, she started to climb off the couch. "I'd better get to bed."

Fred held her. "No, it's all right. Stay here."

"You need your rest."

He didn't, not anymore, but that was beside the point. "Don't worry about it."

He drew her back down to him, and this time she didn't resist. Fred shifted them both downward until their heads reached the pillow, and wedged himself against the back of the sofa, making as much room for her as possible. In a moment her head rested on his chest just below his shoulder, a perfect fit.

From the silence that followed, at first he thought she'd fallen asleep again. Then she raised her head and stared down at him in the dimness, her soft, light hair tumbling around her face. "Fred?"

"What, darling?"

"In the movies"—she passed a hand through her hair—"when something like this is over, nobody remembers what happened."

"This isn't a movie, my love."

It wasn't quite an answer, and she knew it. Lindsay persisted. "Do you think—"

"No." He looked into sleep-confused gray eyes and spoke from his heart. "I couldn't bear you forgetting me. And I could never forget you."

"How do you know?"

He mustered up all the conviction he could. "I'll see to it. I promise."

She rested her head against him once more with a deep sigh. A few minutes later, her steady breathing told him she'd fallen back asleep. He didn't know if his answer had satisfied her or not.

It was as close to lying to Lindsay as he'd ever come. Because, unless he could make it happen through sheer force of will, Fred had no idea whether he'd be able to keep his promise.

Chapter 13

Lindsay woke up alone on the couch.

She jerked upright. She'd fallen asleep with her head resting on Fred's chest. She couldn't imagine how he'd gotten up without dumping her on the floor, much less without waking her.

"Fred?" No answer.

With growing unease, Lindsay pushed the tangled blankets aside and got up to search the apartment. Fred's wet clothes, the ones she'd left draped over the backs of her kitchen chairs two nights ago, were gone. She caught her breath, fighting the beginnings of panic. December twenty-fourth, the day before Christmas. He shouldn't be gone yet. Or had his mysterious powers-that-be decided his job was done?

The knob of her front door turned, and Lindsay held on to the white-runged back of the chair beside her.

Fred walked in, resplendent once again in his

coat, top hat, even carrying the slightly bent walking stick, which Lindsay had almost forgotten. She gripped the chair tighter, fighting the urge to run at him like a flustered housewife from some old TV show.

Fred's eyebrows raised at the sight of her, then lowered in concern as he took in her expression. He strode across the room to her, pulling off his hat as he walked. "I'm sorry. I expected to be back before you were awake."

"It's okay." Lindsay made herself let go of the chair. "After all, why shouldn't you"—*vanish without a trace?*—"go out for—" For what? The newspaper?

"I checked in at Headquarters. I thought you'd prefer I came and went through the door." Fred put his arm around her. She rested her cheek against the front of his crisp white shirt, and touched the lapel of his overcoat. The rough, yet supple texture felt like new, even though she was sure the heavy wool still ought to be damp after being so thoroughly soaked.

"What did they say? At Headquarters?"

"We're back on track. No harm done." Fred reached around her to deposit his hat on the seat of the chair next to her. The hat, like the coat, showed no sign of ever having been dunked in a lake.

"So everything's back to normal." Lindsay tried to keep the disappointment out of her voice. She should know better than to think anything would change. Fred had made that clear last night.

"You could say that. It was a short meeting." Fred's tone was filled with wry humor. "I didn't want to go into too many details. Now I have a proposition for you. You work today, right?"

She nodded. "Usually they close early on Christmas Eve. But I need to be there."

"Understood." He tilted her chin up so that her eyes met his. "Here's my plan. We spend Christmas Eve together, you and I. But there's to be one rule. Live entirely in the present. No serious talk." She could tell he was biting the inside of his lip. "I imagine that's going to be a challenge for you. Think you can manage it?"

"What about S—"

He laid his finger over her lips. "And *absolutely* no mention of what's-his-name. He gets you soon enough. If that's what you decide. Tonight it's just you and I. Are you agreeable?"

One more night of living in the present. Lindsay reached up and put her arms around him, standing on tiptoe to get closer. When her cheek brushed Fred's, the skin against hers was, once again, smooth and clean-shaven.

Lindsay had eaten a few holiday dinners at restaurants before, and they'd always felt a little strange. Tonight, with Fred, was no exception. Until now, she'd never had trouble finding anything to say to him, or felt pressure to make small talk. Tonight was different. For one thing, it was hard to avoid anything that might be construed as serious. In some ways, it felt like a first date.

Fred contributed to the feeling—and, thankfully, to the small talk—by keeping up a constant barrage of questions. He seemed determined to learn everything about her in the short time they had left.

"McDonald's," Lindsay answered. "I was a fry cook." She smiled bemusedly. "I don't get it. How much *do* you know about me? The first night we met, you even knew where to find the nutmeg."

"Parlor tricks. They only told me enough to get you to listen to me. The rest, as you'll recall, I had to learn the hard way."

Fred might find her an endlessly fascinating subject, but Lindsay was getting a little sick of herself. "Your turn," she said. "Tell me something about *you* for a change."

"Ask away. I'm an open book."

Lindsay squinted up at the tulip-shaped lights that hung over their table. Hard to think of a question for someone without a past. "Okay," she floundered. "Your favorite Christmas carol."

"Depends. When I'm in a quiet mood, Handel's

Messiah. When I'm in a festive mood . . . let's see. Maybe 'Carol of the Bells.'"

Lindsay laughed. "You've got to be kidding. That one sounds like Edgar Allan Poe having a nervous breakdown."

"But he did, didn't he? Maybe Christmas drove him to it. Maybe he was just like you, so wrapped up in trying to buy presents and mail cards, he finally snapped, threw up his hands, and said—"

Lindsay groaned as she joined him: "Nevermore."

She shook her head in amazement. Fred's education might be incomplete, but it was certainly varied.

"I hope that's changed for you," he said. "About celebrating Christmas. Next year, don't forget what you've learned. Play the carols, drink the eggnog. Remember what Christmas is about, and what it's for. I want that happiness for you."

This veered dangerously close to serious talk, and Fred seemed to know it. He turned his attention back to his plate. He didn't eat Christmas dinner like anyone else Lindsay had ever seen. Most people launched into the familiar favorites with gusto. Fred was more inclined to sample a bite as though considering it carefully before he moved on to the next item on his plate. His dinner was vanishing, slowly but surely, but he rarely seemed to eat the same thing for two bites in a row.

She waited until he finished a bite of sweet potatoes. "How's the dinner? Is it what you expected?"

"If it makes any sense, it's what I expected, only much more so. I've known intellectually what a Christmas dinner is like, but it's nothing like experiencing it first hand." He sliced into a piece of turkey with exquisitely browned skin. "Have you ever cooked a turkey?"

"A few times, when I've had my parents down. I always need help with the gravy, though." She stirred the light brown, slightly thin mixture poured into the hollow on top of her potatoes. "This is fine. But it can't touch my mother's gravy."

His eyes were thoughtful. "I'll bet she's a lot like you."

"I guess so." Lindsay grinned. "She says it took her ten years to get the recipe right."

"That definitely sounds like you."

"You could find out." Lindsay raised a forkful of non-homemade mashed potatoes and tried to sound casual. "I'd love it if you'd come with me to my parents' house tomorrow."

Fred looked touched, and something else. He avoided her eyes—something Lindsay had come to recognize as a bad sign—and toyed with his glass of sparkling cider. "That's very nice of you. But how on earth would you explain me to your parents?"

"The same way I did at work, I guess. You're visiting from out of the country. . . ."

His eyes met hers again, his gaze so direct it was almost like a stab. "My love, I won't be here tomorrow."

Lindsay's fork froze on its way to her mouth. "What?"

"Come Christmas Day, you're on your own. It's time for you to start applying what you've learned. That's the way it works."

Her appetite vanished. By now, she wouldn't have thought it was possible to feel betrayed by Fred, but she did. "Why didn't you tell me before?"

"I didn't want you thinking about it." Fred took her hand, lightly tracing her knuckle. "We have until midnight tonight."

"That means we've only got—"

Lindsay looked down at her wrist, but not before Fred laid his hand over her watch, then neatly slipped it off in one smooth motion. He put it in his pocket. "Forgive me. But this is what I wanted to avoid. If you have it on, you'll keep looking at it."

"There's that candlelight service at eleven—"

"I'll make sure we don't miss it. For the rest of the night, when it comes to time, you're on a need-to-know basis."

* * *

She would have thought Fred wouldn't want to go anywhere near the lake, so soon after having been under it. But when she told him that was the neighborhood with the best Christmas lights, he was the one who suggested making the short trip up the mountain.

After surveying several streets from the car, Lindsay parked near the pier on the south side, where the lake was ringed by two-story homes with colorful lights that cast blurred reflections on the frozen water. Lindsay felt her eyes pulled toward the north end of the lake, where Fred had taken his spill, but it was too far away to see.

They got out of her car and walked alongside the lake, where flat boards over the edge of the water replaced ordinary sidewalks. If she'd been with anyone else, Lindsay would have been freezing. But with Fred beside her, she'd long since discovered, she was never cold.

They stopped and rested their arms on the rough wooden railing that bordered the walkway. Lindsay's eyes skimmed over the houses, especially the ones with lighted Christmas trees downstairs and darkened windows upstairs, where the children's bedrooms would be. She could feel the descending quiet, the growing anticipation. And tried to fight her own increasing dread. They had so little time left. She shivered despite the fact that she wasn't cold.

Fred put his arm around her. "So, what do you think is happening in these houses tonight?"

"The children are nestled all snug in their beds?"

"Of course. But what's going on in, say, that house?" He pointed to a home where every tree and bush was wrapped or covered in red and green lights. "I say Mom and Dad have put the children to bed. She's wrapping the last of the presents, and he's trying to assemble a tricycle."

Just when she thought she'd gotten used to Fred . . . Lindsay turned with a frown. "How do you know that?"

He chuckled. "I don't. It's just a game. You can do it too. How about—say, that house?"

He pointed to one trimmed in white icicle lights. Through a downstairs window, Lindsay glimpsed the flickering blue eye of a television screen. "They're watching *It's a Wonderful Life*."

"Quite possible. But you can do better. Try again. Use what you *don't* see."

Lindsay contemplated a solemn, blue-lit nativity scene in front of another house. An older couple, probably, she decided, and tried to picture the scenario inside. "They're roasting a turkey in the oven overnight," she said. "The house is going to smell incredible in the morning."

"You see? Very good."

Lindsay spotted a yard full of Charlie Brown figures painted on plywood. Definitely kids in that house. Her eyes lingered on Snoopy. "They're getting a puppy."

"Perfect." His arm tightened around her. "That's something else I don't know about you. Did you ever get a puppy for Christmas?"

"Not for Christmas. We always had pets, though."

"Was there ever anything special you wanted for Christmas, but you never got?"

She couldn't help it. She turned to Fred again and stared at him for several long, slow beats. *No serious talk,* she reminded herself. So she didn't say it.

Lindsay searched her memory for something else. "Ballet slippers."

"Oh?"

Lindsay shrugged. "It was kind of silly. I never even asked my parents for lessons, let alone the shoes. I was never too athletic."

"Is that the point? You know, there are very few accomplished ballerinas. But I'm sure for every one of them, there must be thousands of others who love to dance."

He was reading too much into this. "It's not some big unresolved thing," she protested. "It was just a whim. I wouldn't have been any good at it."

"Whims are fine. I just don't like the idea of your believing you wouldn't be 'good enough' at anything." He tucked a strand of hair behind her ear. "You don't have to do everything *right*, Lindsay."

Fred studied her thoughtfully, and she squirmed.

"That's what you've been doing all along, isn't it? This is the time of year when you made your worst mistake. And you've been trying to make up for it ever since. That's why you're always trying so hard to get Christmas *right*. And that's why you miss out."

So Fred, the amateur psychologist, had finally hit the nail on the head. Or at least, he'd come close.

Lindsay attempted a casual tone. "Pretty obvious, isn't it?"

"Was it obvious to you?"

"No," she admitted. But an unwelcome thought snaked in under her skin. Last night and several times today, she'd entertained a wish that was every bit as unlikely as her becoming a prima ballerina. The idea that some divine agency would ever let her keep someone like Fred. She didn't deserve Fred, any more than she ever would have been able to dance in those shoes.

Useless, self-pitying thoughts. She wouldn't let them ruin her last night with Fred; not just for herself, but for him. "Okay. You win. You get your degree in amateur psychology." She smiled up at him. "But it sounds an awful lot like serious talk to me."

"You're right. I should be flogged." He took her

hand and started toward the car. "Now, we'd better start back down the hill for that church service."

Fred slipped his fingers through Lindsay's, marveling again at what a natural fit it seemed to make. He started to put their hands into his pocket, then reached into the wide, deep pocket of Lindsay's red coat instead. Something scratched at the bottom of the pocket, and he smiled at the memory. "Chestnut shells."

Her fingers squeezed between his. "I guess it's the first time I've worn this coat since that night."

Somehow, in less than a week and a half, they'd developed a history. At least, it seemed that way to him. Maybe he was just breaking his own rule against being serious, giving everything a heightened meaning tonight. Like the way it had become second nature to match his pace to hers as they walked, slowing his longer strides when he felt Lindsay begin to quicken her steps to keep up.

Time might be limited, but nothing should feel rushed.

At the car, he opened her door and kissed her cheek as she got inside. He used the brief trip around to his own door to draw some vigor from the cold air around him, and the strength to keep the mood light. At first, he'd tried to pull back tonight, not to touch her too much, thinking it might make matters easier to get back on a more casual footing before he left. He wouldn't be seeing her again, and he might as well get used to it.

But he'd have far too much time to get used to it. Where he went from here, and how long his kind lived, he didn't know. But without Lindsay, it would seem a very long time indeed.

Did other people form deep attachments this quickly? Or was everything compressed for him because his time with her was so short? For Lindsay, this period would probably soon seem like a brief anomaly, a small pocket of time separate from her real, day-to-day life. If she remembered it at all.

He thought of his promise, and resolved with all his might to make sure it came true.

A heavy sigh from Lindsay mirrored his thoughts. He had to be careful. Moods were contagious, and he was a carrier now. Another sign, he supposed, that he'd been here as long as he ought to be.

Time for a diversion.

He pulled up straighter in his seat as the church came into view. "We're early," he said. "Park around the corner."

"Why?" Lindsay glanced toward the little digital clock on the lower half of the dashboard, but he kept his knee steadfastly in front of it, the way he had all evening. His legs didn't fit in many other places in this car, as it was.

"Trust me. I'm in charge, remember?"

A little suspicion glinted in her smile, and she parked the car near an evergreen tree alongside the road, where the tree cast a slightly darker shadow.

Fred unfastened her safety belt and reached across her waist. "How does your seat adjust?"

"What?" He'd already found the lever, and the seat fell ungracefully backward, taking Lindsay with it. But grace wasn't the object here. The less serious, the better. Fred leaned awkwardly over her, fumbling for a position, tangling his hands through her hair, breathing lightly across her ear.

Her giggle was music to his ears. "Fred, we can't—"

"Don't worry. Even I can't get us into much trouble in five minutes."

He moved his lips downward, gently nudging aside the neck of her sweater to nuzzle the soft skin at the side of her throat, until the giggling quieted. Then he kissed her, long and full.

Slowly. He refused to hurry anything tonight. Her arms came up around him as she responded, drawing him deeper into that incredible sensation of warmth, of being connected.

When words failed, there was this. Even with so little time left, her kiss took him to a place where he couldn't even think anymore. Nothing but the two of them, joined together in a moment so perfect everything else ceased to exist.

In Lindsay's arms, five minutes was a very short time indeed. Just enough to lose himself completely, only to have to drag himself back again.

He propped himself up precariously on the corner of Lindsay's headrest, pulling away just far enough to look down into her eyes, nearly lost in the shadows. "We should be going inside now," he said unnecessarily.

Lindsay nodded, fingering his chin, which he knew was as smooth as it had been this morning. He couldn't read her thoughts and he shouldn't want to. But he could guess. He would have liked to have those bristles back too, if it meant he could stay with her.

The church clock began to strike eleven. Only one hour left.

"Now look what you've done. Made us late." Fred smiled down at her with a lightness he didn't feel, and got out to open the door for her.

The church Lindsay had chosen was small and placid, and Fred felt something settle inside him as soon as he entered. It was the right place for him to be now, to remember that there were things much larger than his own problems. The age-old holiday had existed long before him, and would continue to do so long after these small, earthly issues were forgotten.

Still. He was, for the moment, flesh and blood,

and he would accept that for the gift it was. These final moments shouldn't be wasted.

So, with his arm around Lindsay, he sang along with the old traditional songs, songs he knew without ever having learned them. When he touched his candle to hers, he prayed he was passing something more on to her than just a flame. And he walked outside with her, their candles still lit, keeping firmly focused on the fast-waning present.

The candlelight service was short, and Lindsay's apartment was just a few minutes away. In spite of that, it was all she could do to keep from speeding on the way home. Fred rested a hand on her leg. "It's all right. We still have fifteen minutes."

Fifteen minutes? How could he be so calm? His knee still blocked her view of the clock on the dashboard. But at least his touch reassured her that he was still there. That made it a little easier to keep her eyes on the road.

When they reached her front porch, Lindsay started to open the door, but Fred rested a hand on hers. "This is where I leave you."

Lindsay swallowed hard and turned around to face him. Not much point wasting time trying to talk him into coming inside for a cup of coffee. She fixed her gaze on him, trying to take in every detail of his features. Fred seemed to be doing the same thing. No man on earth, she was sure, could ever match the way his dark eyes looked at her.

Don't let me forget, she thought.

Fred stepped close and rested a hand on her cheek. His eyes left hers briefly to glance around the porch area, illuminated by its lone, diamond-shaped lamp. "You'll hang some lights outside next year, won't you? Wherever you are?"

It sounded a little too much like a last request. Lindsay nodded, not trusting her voice.

"I don't know what to say." Fred's voice brushed against her ears, always a wonderful sound, perhaps a bit huskier than usual. "So maybe I'll just give you your Christmas present."

From the pocket of his overcoat, he slid out a long, narrow box, neatly packaged in gift wrap Lindsay recognized from the supply in her closet.

"Fred, you didn't have to."

"I wanted to."

She gave up arguing. They didn't have time for that. Lindsay tore away the paper and beheld a jewelry store box, warped and discolored with signs of water damage. Her breath drew in sharply.

"Sorry," Fred said. "It went in the lake with me. But the contents held up surprisingly well."

She remembered the way Fred had asked about his coat the next morning. It had seemed like such an odd non sequitur at the time. Now, with trembling hands, she opened the water-stained

221

cardboard box. Inside was a second, hard-shelled box. And inside that box, a delicate gold wristwatch, the crystal over its face showing the faintest remainder of mist.

"It's still running," he said.

Lindsay could see that. The tiny gold second hand traveled around a slender, oval face. It read five minutes to twelve.

Fred turned the watch over on its velvet bed. At first she thought he was trying to hide the time from her, but then she saw the inscription on the back. Lindsay angled it under the porch light and read, "No Time Like The Present."

"Did I do all right?" Fred sounded concerned.

You can do this. Don't cry in front of him. "It's perfect. Thank you."

He held her, and she clung, hard, to the back of his neck. She didn't want to let go, and she didn't want him to see the tears starting to leak from the corners of her eyes.

"Shh." He didn't seem to realize he held her waist as tightly as she was holding on to him. "It's all for a reason, my love."

He pulled her back to look at her. The outside of his fingertips touched her face. "Lindsay, I—" He broke off. "You're lovely. Did you know that?"

She shook her head mutely, the ache in her throat too huge for her to talk around it.

"Never forget it. The man who gets you is a lucky

man indeed." His voice dropped. "There's one more thing for you in the bottom of the box."

Lindsay lifted away the velvet backing with care. At the bottom of the box, she saw something small and white. A slip of paper. Written on it, in neat script, was Steven's name, with an address below it.

Her stomach muscles tightened. "How did you get this?"

"Headquarters. Although I suspect you could have gotten the same information from a telephone directory."

The address was in Durango, about half an hour from her parents' house. Lindsay stared at the handwriting on the slip, presumably Fred's. She'd never seen his writing before.

"He'd better deserve you," Fred said suddenly, his voice returning to nearly its normal tone. "Or I'm coming back next year. As a vengeful spirit. Yowling, clanking chains, the whole bit."

She hugged him again, with all her strength. Something somewhere between a laugh and a sob caught in her throat. Fred seemed to have that effect on her.

"It doesn't make any sense," she said.

"It's what's best for you." His words were buried in her hair. "They're never wrong."

"They are this time," she whispered fiercely.

He kissed her, and she knew this one had to be the last. Lindsay held on tight, not wanting it to end. She felt a world of longing behind it; any of Fred's pretense of not being serious was gone. He raised his lips from hers slowly, not letting go of her, his eyes heavy on hers.

She had to say it. Why hadn't she said it before? "Fred, I—"

He released her and stepped back, outside the dim ring of her porch light. And for the first time tonight, Lindsay felt the bitter bite of the winter air around her.

"You don't need to say it." His voice sounded strained, and somehow fainter.

Tears blurred her vision. She sensed, rather than saw, Fred take one more step back.

His words seemed to come from far away: "I love you, too."

Lindsay blinked her eyes hard to clear them, and when she opened them, she was standing alone on the porch.

Where Fred had stood, and out in the night beyond, a fine, white snow began to fall.

Chapter 14

On Christmas morning, Lindsay woke up with a broken heart.

She couldn't look at a single thing in her apartment that didn't remind her of Fred. The Christmas decorations. The toaster. The couch where he'd so often draped his overcoat. And if she closed her eyes, she smelled the pine fragrance of the tree he'd brought her. It looked and smelled as fresh now as it had the day they put it up.

Even last night's light dusting of snow—enough to decorate lawns, bushes and trees, but not enough to stick to the pavement—bore testimony to Fred's promise of a white Christmas.

Everything made her think of Fred. But that was better than forgetting.

So she wore the watch, packed a bag, and drove the nearly empty highway to her parents' house, with presents in the trunk and Steven's address, like a lump of burning coal, in her pocket.

Her mother loved the glass deer from the street fair. And if she noticed anything amiss in her daughter's behavior, she was tactful enough not to mention it. When Lindsay was with her mother and father, when she was busy, sometimes she felt almost normal. Almost. When she was alone, and had time to think, the hurt seemed to be there waiting for her, like prickles of barbed wire.

The Saturday after Christmas, Lindsay made the drive to Durango, and Steven. It still didn't feel right. But Fred had asked her to. And, though he hadn't seemed concerned about it, she wasn't sure what might happen to him if she didn't.

The directions she'd gotten online brought her to a pretty little gray house on a quiet suburban street. The bare branches of a willow tree formed a huge, bony umbrella over most of the front yard. In the summer, the shade must be lovely. The place seemed warm and homey enough, not unlike the neighborhood where they'd grown up.

A dark blue sedan sat in the driveway, so Lindsay parked at the curb. It would be just her luck to scrape her ex-boyfriend's fender before he ever laid eyes on her again.

Ex-boyfriend. And once, for a few days, he'd been her fiancé.

Lindsay pried her hands from their tenacious grip on the steering wheel, got out of the car, and walked up to the doorstep. It looked as if they hadn't had snow here in the past week. She knew her parents hadn't. Everything just looked brown and wet, except for the sky, heavy with gray clouds. She'd chosen a gloomy day to do this, but she figured Saturday was the most likely day to catch him at home.

She stood, hand poised over the doorbell, wondering why she hadn't called first.

Because Fred's slip of paper had included an address, but not a telephone number. On the phone, it would be easy for Steven to tell her not to come, and give her a coward's way out. Again. It was much harder to turn someone away when they were already standing on your front porch.

Lindsay stopped trying to gather her courage. She'd never be ready enough. She rang the bell, remembering the first time she'd sold Girl Scout cookies as a child. Back then, she'd ring the doorbell and wait nervously for a few seconds. *Not home? Oh, too bad.* She'd turn to leave, and then the door would open.

Today she held her ground, though retreat still sounded tremendously tempting. The door opened.

A very recognizable Steven stood framed in the doorway, wearing jeans and a red sweater. His face had lost that adolescent leanness, taking on a more adult look, but he wore the last ten years well. She would have recognized him anywhere.

Familiar blue eyes stared at her as if an ostrich had appeared on his porch. "Lindsay?"

She'd thought of about eighty things to say on the drive up, and none of them were any good. "Hi," she began.

A little girl, about four years old, appeared beside him. Standing close to Steven's leg, she peered at Lindsay curiously. "Who is it, Daddy?"

Lindsay's mind raced as she looked down into the brown eyes of the little girl. Maybe this was beginning to make sense. If this little girl needed a mother—

"Sweetie, come back and finish your lunch." A pretty blond woman joined the little girl beside Steven, and looked questioningly at Lindsay with the same brown eyes as the child. "Hi." She scooped the girl up.

This didn't add up. Lindsay knew she was far from perfect, but a home wrecker she wasn't. And surely Headquarters didn't intend that, either. So why had they sent her here?

Steven still stared at her. She wasn't sure if he'd blinked yet. "Honey, this is Lindsay."

"Oh." Clearly, the woman had heard of her. Lindsay prayed for a crack in the pavement to slither into.

"Lindsay, this is my wife, Karen, and our daughter, Hannah."

A world of questions lay behind those introductions. Lindsay said inanely, "Nice to meet you."

Karen said, "Let her in, sweetie. It must be freezing out there."

Oh, great. The gray, overcast day only made her look piteous.

"Sure. Sorry." Steven stepped aside, and Lindsay walked in, wondering why she was here and not the moon.

Karen hitched Hannah up on her hip. She was the kind of woman who could take five seconds to twist her hair up loosely into a clip, the way it was now, and look fabulous. "Can I get you anything? Some coffee?"

Oh. No. Weird. Way too weird. "No, thanks. I just dropped by for a minute." *To humiliate myself.*

"Oh." A perfect blond strand fell loosely over Karen's eyebrow, and she tilted her head to move it aside. "Well, I was just trying to get Hannah to finish her lunch, so . . ."

Karen nodded with a vague smile and headed off through a doorway to the left, with Hannah peering back over her shoulder at Lindsay. Obviously a secure woman. But then, what could Lindsay possibly do? Run off with her husband?

Steven motioned her in the opposite direction, toward the living room. Lindsay took a seat on the couch, while he sat in an armchair facing her. The look of bewilderment had never left his face. "Excuse the mess."

The Christmas tree stood framed in the window, the carpet around it littered with Barbies, stuffed animals, and some new-looking furry pink slippers. It looked just the way a little girl's living room should look three days after Christmas. "No, it's fine."

Lindsay searched for some proof that she was still able to put together a coherent sentence. She closed her eyes and tried to equate this baffled stranger with the person she'd known so well, so many years ago. "Steven, this is really dumb. I'm not even sure why I'm here."

Fred's words echoed in her memory: *Make it right.*

"I guess it's to apologize. And maybe explain."

"You don't have to do that." His blue eyes made a perfect mirror—cool, opaque, and much harder to read than Fred's. "It was a long time ago."

"I know." Lindsay searched her mind, trying to come up with some sort of explanation that didn't involve angels or Headquarters or getting herself carted away on that overdue trip to Bellevue. She didn't want to seem any more crazy or pitiful than she already did.

All she could come up with was the truth. "If there's anything I've ever done that I wish I'd done differently—that's it. And I'm sorry. For the way I handled it, I mean. I just wasn't ready, and I didn't have the guts to tell you. I don't think I knew what I wanted."

Steven leaned forward, resting his elbows on his knees, a posture that reminded her more of the person she used to know. "To tell you the truth, I kind of wondered if I was supposed to go after you. Like it was some kind of test. I thought maybe that was what you wanted, but . . ."

Fred would have come after me. As if it made any difference. "But you didn't."

"No. I can't remember now if I was more hurt or more ticked off." He gave her a curious half-smile. "This isn't some kind of twelve-step thing, is it? Like Alcoholics Anonymous, where you go back to people you—"

"No." Lindsay's face scorched. But she'd come this far and endured this much. This was one thing she was going to do right. She eyed the tree. "I didn't ruin Christmas for you, did I?"

He chuckled. "Well, the first year afterward was nothing to write home about. But no." He nodded toward the indistinct sound of voices from the other side of the house. "Things turned out fine. In fact—"

He leaned forward and reached down to pull up a branch near the bottom of the tree, to display an ornament Lindsay had almost forgotten. A ridiculous purple cow. She'd given it to him, probably their junior year, as a joke. It was even more hideous than she remembered.

She remembered Fred's words: *Some of the best Christmas decorations are hideous.*

"You still have that thing? You've got to be kidding."

"Hannah loves it. She has to be the one to hang it, every year."

Lindsay listened to a rhythmic clatter, somewhere behind her, of silverware banging out an improvised pattern against a plate. "You just have the one?"

"So far."

"She's beautiful," Lindsay said. "They both are."

She prodded herself for any sign of jealousy, but couldn't find any, unless it was in the notion that the little girl might have been hers.

"I'm happy for you," she said. "I really am." And found she meant it.

Steven sat back a little, his face relaxing into a more natural smile. "That's really all you came for?"

She shrugged. "That's it."

"Well, you didn't have to. But it was nice of you."

Lindsay couldn't think of anything else to say, but something in her lightened. She felt a sense of completeness.

Reconciled. Belatedly, comprehension of the word hit her. Fred hadn't been sent to reunite her with

Steven permanently; just to resolve her unfinished business.

Headquarters could have saved them both a lot of pain if they'd just *said* that.

"What about you?" Steven was saying. "Are you married?"

"No. Not yet," she bluffed.

She wondered now if it would ever happen for her. It had never been an everyday preoccupation for her, but now . . .

Lindsay pulled herself to her feet. "I'd better be going."

A chapter of her life had been put to rest. But the rest lay before her, an unfinished book.

"You must be having one lousy vacation," Jeanne said. "If I was off work, I wouldn't come within ten miles of here."

They sat in the Thai restaurant across the street from the office, two days after Lindsay's visit to Steven. "It's been a strange Christmas," she admitted.

These days, Lindsay knew Jeanne better than Steven, but she still couldn't think where to start. But if Jeanne could learn anything from her mistake, it would be worth it. She waited until their coconut soup arrived before she started beating around the bush in earnest.

"Jeanne—" Lindsay poked a mushroom down into her soup. "This is none of my business, but I wanted to talk to you. About Brad. I could be totally wrong, and you can tell me to—"

"Brad?" Jeanne snorted and jabbed two skinny red straws into her Thai iced tea. "Don't even mention the name."

Lindsay raised her head. "Cubic zirconia?" she said before she thought.

"It might as well have been. The day after Christmas, he started making noise about how short he was on cash. And he never took his eyes off my finger."

"So what did you do?"

Jeanne held her bare left hand over the table with a dismissive flicking motion. "Told him to take a walk."

"Oh." If Lindsay had been less distracted, she would have noticed the ring was gone.

"Why? What were you going to say?"

"It doesn't matter. I just—" There was no need to go on. Jeanne's problem had already been solved, and she seemed to be holding up surprisingly well.

"No, really. Did you know something I didn't?"

Lindsay combed her fingers through her hair. "Like I said, it was none of my business. But I was worried about you. When you showed me the ring, you just looked a little—"

"Green around the gills?"

Lindsay nodded.

"You know who really looked green? Brad, when he was trying to worm out. I guess I was kind of relieved." Jeanne set down her spoon, and Lindsay realized the other woman hadn't started on her soup. "I never should have said yes in the first place. I shouldn't be that anxious to get married. But when someone asks—I don't know, I guess I felt like it might be my only chance."

"I felt that way, too."

Jeanne's head lifted.

"I was engaged once. Back in college. Not for very long. But that's what I wanted to tell you. After I said yes, I had this feeling in my stomach—"

"Like you swallowed something and it was sitting there like a rock?"

"That's it. And I thought maybe you felt the same way. I didn't want to butt in if it was what you really wanted, but I felt bad not saying anything." Lindsay stopped. She was babbling again. She seemed to be doing a lot of babbling these days.

"You're a good friend, Lindsay." Jeanne stirred her iced tea. "And here I didn't even know you'd ever been engaged. How come we never do anything away from the office?"

"I don't know."

"Come to my New Year's party tomorrow night. You always say you'll try, but you never make it."

"You're still having it?"

"Sure." Jeanne finally took a spoonful of her soup. "I'm not in mourning. I just feel kind of stupid." She smiled. "If you really want to cheer me up, bring a batch of that fudge. The almond kind. It was awesome last time."

Lindsay's eyes stung unexpectedly. She leaned over her soup, and felt Jeanne's suddenly watchful eyes.

"Hey. How about you? Whatever happened with the merry Englishman?"

Lindsay studied floating bits of parsley. "He's gone."

"The rat."

"No, it's not like that. He didn't have a choice. He—"

He disappeared off my doorstep.

The reality, or the unreality, of it hit her again full force. Lindsay set down her spoon and closed her eyes tight for a moment, then looked at Jeanne desperately. At least Jeanne remembered him too.

"You saw him, didn't you?" Lindsay asked, just to be sure. "You thought he was—"

"Six feet of gorgeous. And nuts about you."

"Thanks." Lindsay dabbed at her eyes with a wry smile. "I'm not sure if that helps or not."

"I'm sorry," Jeanne said. "I shouldn't have called him a rat. I didn't mean it. Sometimes it's easier to get mad than—"

"I know." If Fred had done anything wrong, maybe that would help. Instead, she clung to a perfect image of the way he'd looked at her, those last few minutes at her front door.

Lindsay took a deep swig of her tea. When she set her glass down, Jeanne was studying her intently.

"Oh, honey. You're worse off than I am. I didn't know." Lindsay's eyes blurred. "You feel like *this,* and you come down and take me to lunch because you're worried about *me* getting hurt? We shouldn't be having lunch. We should be out knocking back mai tais, or one of those dumb little drinks with umbrellas."

Lindsay sputtered out a laugh. "And singing karaoke."

"Say you'll come tomorrow night. You need it."

Lindsay nodded. "Okay. I'll tr—"

Jeanne raised an eyebrow in warning.

"I'll be there," Lindsay amended.

Chapter 15

Lindsay stood near the big plate of cheese and crackers on Jeanne's dining room table, sipping tentatively from her plastic stemware glass. Jeanne took great pride in the fact that she had successfully duplicated Phil and Helen's pineapple punch, and Lindsay didn't want another sugar-induced headache. The volume in the tiny apartment threatened to do that anyway. Lots of voices, competing with the background music, a CD shuffle of Christmas songs having their last hurrah for the year.

Whatever Jeanne's troubles with men, there were certainly enough of them at her party, and they had a definite tendency to swarm around their hostess. Lindsay smiled as she saw Matt try to get a word in edgewise as Jeanne chatted with someone tall, blond and handsome.

I was right, she thought. *I've got to tell Fred.*

And winced inside. She wondered when thoughts like that would stop coming so often.

She'd ventured out tonight, she supposed, mostly for him. It would be tempting, and easy, to curl up into a ball and stay home. But she knew Fred wouldn't have wanted that. He'd talked so often about wanting to leave her with something positive. So she'd worn her red sweater, trying to look festive for one last holiday fling, and she'd come.

At least she could make it better than that *other* New Year's Eve ten years ago.

She looked for someone to talk to. Some of the people, she knew from the office; most, she didn't. Lindsay smiled vacantly and moved back toward the living room, determined not to stay anchored in one spot all night. Maybe she could keep Matt company for a little while, or find someone who wanted to talk about the hors d'oeuvres.

And then she saw him.

Someone else must have let him in, because Jeanne was still surrounded by her clutch of men. Lindsay blinked hard, in case her eyes were playing a trick on her. She bit her tongue hard, in case she was dreaming. Because there, fifteen feet across the room, was Fred Holliday.

And yet it wasn't. No overcoat, no top hat, not even an undersize sweatshirt, just black slacks and a dark green sweater she'd never seen before, the kind you'd see at any present-day department store.

He looked ever so slightly out of place, as though he were searching for someone.

He glanced in her direction, and her heart seemed to stop.

He didn't recognize her. For a moment she was sure of it. His face was so utterly still, Lindsay couldn't read any expression there.

Then he started toward her with a smooth, purposeful stride, so purposeful that other people in the room automatically moved aside. As he got closer, she could see just how intently his dark eyes were fixed on her. What she'd mistaken for lack of expression had been intense focus. Lindsay became aware that her heart was, in fact, beating; more than that, it was pounding. And that she should be moving too, instead of standing as if her knees had been replaced by sacks of wet cement.

When she started toward Fred, other people moved out of the way for her too. She couldn't remember that ever happening before.

And they crushed together, arms locked around each other so tightly Lindsay couldn't breathe and didn't care. All she could do was hold on. He was here. He was solid. He was real.

Standing on tiptoe, she hung her chin over his shoulder. "I thought you evaporated," she whispered.

"I'm not sure you were wrong."

She pulled back, just enough to give him a questioning stare.

241

Fred smiled. "Is there a place we can talk alone?"

Lindsay cast her eyes around, and they fell on the sliding glass patio door at the back of the room. Taking Fred's hand, she led him toward it. By the time they reached the door, Jeanne stood there waiting with a knowing smile, and pulled it open for them. They stepped out onto a little concrete balcony, about four feet wide.

Before the glass door finished sliding shut, Fred had her in his arms again, lifting her off her feet as his mouth covered hers. Lindsay dangled in space, pressed against him, feeling a heady, floating sensation as he turned them in a small, slow circle on the tiny balcony. It was Fred, all right, marvelously unchanged, despite the external differences.

Not until he set her down, raining kisses over her face, did she begin to feel the cold. They'd had no snow in the past week, but the night was brittle and still. Only the lack of any wind made it bearable to stand out here without a jacket.

"Well, we'll have privacy for certain." Fred clasped his arms loosely around her waist, holding her securely to him. "It's freezing out here."

Fred, cold? She looked up at him. "Freezing?"

"Yes, I assure you, I'm very mortal. Now."

"H-how? Is that good or bad?"

"I suppose that depends on you." His eyes searched her face. "I woke up in a hospital. Amnesia victim."

242

"Amnesia?"

"Think about it. How else would you describe a thirty-year-old man with no memory before the last two weeks or so?" He caressed her hair. "I never forgot about you, or about us. But I couldn't tell them that. I didn't know if you should be involved. I didn't know what the outcome would be with Steven."

"He's married. Happily. With a little girl."

"Good for him." He kissed the top of her head. "Thank you for going. You made this possible."

"How?"

"Well, they found me unconscious, not far from the hospital, on December twenty-eighth. Does that date mean anything to you?"

It was burned into her memory. "It's the day I went to see Steven."

"It's also the birth date on my passport. They found it in my coat pocket. Fred Holliday, Camden Way, London."

Lindsay frowned. "But I made that up."

"And someone else made it so. My supervisors are a very decent lot, really."

Until just now, she'd almost decided they were a bunch of sadists. Lindsay smoothed her hand over the shoulder of his sweater, making sure yet again that he was really there. She ran her finger along the bottom of his jaw. Rough.

"So," he went on, "I made as if I didn't know how

I'd gotten here, which is very nearly the truth. For a while I was afraid they were going to ship me off to live out my days in some little flat in Camden that I'd never seen before. Then, yesterday, a gray-haired gentleman showed up. Him, I recognized."

"From Headquarters?"

He nodded. "One of my supervisors. Only he told them he was my uncle, and they released me to his custody. A very nice man. You've met him, by the way. Threw him out of your apartment, in fact."

Lindsay gasped. "That was your boss?"

"*Was* is the operative word. His last official act was to bring me here to you tonight."

"You're really here for good?"

"Completely earthbound, my dear. And I'm hoping you think it's a good thing."

"Of course it is." It was too wonderful to be true. Maybe that was why she had so much trouble believing it. There had to be a catch. "But *why?*"

He brushed the side of her cheek lightly with cool fingers, and Lindsay reached up and held them. For once, her hands were warmer than his. "Each of us had a job to do," he said. "Mine was to guide you to be reconciled with Steven, and yours was to follow through. To see Steven and free yourself of this idea that you'd done some irreparable damage. That you didn't deserve to be loved. Or even enjoy Christmas."

"So why didn't they *tell* you that?" Lindsay felt a bewildering mixture of joy and exasperation.

"Because, if I was meant for you, I had to want what was best for you. Even if it wasn't what I wanted. They couldn't very well say, 'Do the unselfish thing, and the girl is yours.' That would defeat the purpose. We had to act for the right reasons." He squeezed her hand. "Do you understand it now? Think about it, Lindsay." He took both of her hands in his and gazed into her eyes. "Something like this doesn't happen every day. I was truly made for you."

Dark eyes shone into hers.

"My Christmas present," she whispered.

"Exactly. But first we had to earn it."

"But I don't deserve . . . you . . ."

He placed a finger over her lips. "Don't talk like that. Do you want me to vanish in a puff of smoke?"

Her eyes widened in horror. He laughed.

"Don't worry, darling. I love you and I'm here to stay. Unless you prove me wrong, by breaking my heart and sending me away."

"Never." Finally she could say it. What she hadn't had a chance to say on that last night, when she thought she'd never see him again. "I love you."

She moved toward him again, but with all his resolve, Fred held her back.

It was so hard for him to hold any distance from her at all. He felt beset by warring urges—to look at her, to talk to her, to all but devour her. And the fear that she'd get tired of this, despite the fact that she practically glowed before him. He couldn't believe she was his, and that uncertainty was a new feeling. He seemed to have picked up just a niggling of insecurity. He supposed it came with this mortal body, along with hunger, thirst, and the ability to feel truly cold.

There were so many things to consider. Where he would find gainful employment. How they would live. The practical implications of this were staggering, and he knew he couldn't have thought of even half of them. But that could wait. Now that he'd answered all of her questions, he had only one of his own.

He took a deep breath and asked it. "Lindsay Miller, will you marry me?"

She flung her arms around his neck. "Yes."

From inside the apartment came the distant sound of whoops and horns, welcoming in the new year. Their first holiday season together was complete.

He kissed her, arms closing around her, until both of them forgot the cold. Afterward, Fred drew her closer, and chuckled.

He said, "You'll regret this, you know. And you've got no one to blame but yourself."

"What do you mean?"

"You've just agreed to spend the rest of your life with a man named Fred."

Epilogue

Fred and Lindsay Holliday run a bakery in Lakeside, Colorado, which is renowned for its fudge, especially the recipe with almonds. Their friends, who see them often, say they know how to celebrate the Christmas season better than anyone else they know, a spirit that seems to linger in their household throughout the year.

For Christmas, every year, they send postcards.